MW00618832

THE ASSISTED LIVING
FACILITY LIBRARY

The

Assisted Living Facility

Library

———

Richard Kalich

GREEN INTEGER

KØBENHAVN & LOS ANGELES

2020

GREEN INTEGER
Edited by Per Bregne
København / Los Angeles
(323) 937-3783 / www.greeninteger.com

Distributed in the United States by
Consortium Book Sales & Distribution / Ingram Books
(800) 283-3572 / www.cbsd.com

First Green Integer Edition 2020
Copyright ©2020 by Richard Kalich
Back cover copy ©2020 by Green Integer
All rights reserved

Book Design: Pablo Capra
Cover photograph of Richard Kalich by Kevin Li

LIBRARY OF CONGRESS CATALOGING-IN-PUBLICATION DATA
Richard Kalich [1947]
The Assisted Living Facility Library
ISBN: 978-1-933382-29-6
p. cm—Green Integer 210
I. Title II. Series

Green Integer books are published for Douglas Messerli
Printed in the USA

In appreciation and gratitude to the most generous and giving person I've known in all my years of writing: Brian Evenson.

And a special Thank You to my young neighbor, Bennett Galef, who daily came into my apartment to listen and offer constructive comments as the pages unfolded.

"The novel no longer implies writing about an adventure but recounts the adventure of writing."

JEAN RICARDOU

"The 'being' of 'being a Writer' is extremely unstable and problematic; it's precisely 'being' that the act of writing puts into question."

JEFFREY DESHELL
University of Colorado, Boulder

"Not writing is always a relief and sometimes a pleasure. Writing about what cannot be written, by contrast, is the devil's own job. Yet words on a page make all things possible. Any line, even this one, may be a place to begin."

IVAN VLADISLAVIC
The Loss Library and Other Unfinished Stories

June 18, 2019

Central Park Assisted Living
June Longua, Director
333 Central Park West
New York, New York

Dear Mr. Richard Kalich,

I am taking it upon myself to answer your concerns regarding our Central Park Assisted Living facility. Firstly, as we've already written you in our initial acceptance letter, we would be honored to have you as a resident with us. We combine top-notch healthcare, exciting amenities and dozens of activities into one vibrant lifestyle. Wasn't it you, yourself, who stated that you would be hard pressed to find better retirement accommodations than what Central Park Assisted Living has to offer?

* Assistance with the tasks of daily living
* 24-hour medical and security response

* Emergency response system
* Bathroom pull cords
* Weekly housekeeping
* Full-time Board-Certified Geriatrician Medical Director
* Wheelchair-accessible transportation

And in addition to a relatively independent lifestyle and active life, you will experience the peace of mind knowing that continuing care is available—should you need it in the future.

However, as much as we would be glad to welcome you (a bed will be made ready within a two-week notification for the next one year), there is one small caveat I must address: Though Assisted Living residences are approximately 400 square feet, each with a private bathroom and shower, there is just no way we can accommodate your request to house your library of 10,000 books. Our residences simply do not have the space. Not to mention that it would be a fire hazard. Still, if you would kindly allow me to make a suggestion: Would you be amenable to selecting one hundred (100) books from your library, perhaps from those "favorite bookshelves" you mentioned to me personally and so lovingly on the date of your last visit? That would solve our dilemma.

Of course, in the future you could exchange or rotate the hundred books to your heart's content.

I want to personally thank you for your understanding and cooperation. If further information is needed, please do not hesitate to call me at 646-8748, extension 8736.

Sincerely Yours,
June Longua, Director

Where did this come from? Who knew you had this inside you?

Those were the first words Kalich's twin brother said to him after having read his novel *The Nihilesthete*. What made them resonate inside Kalich for the next thirty-five years was not only that he was Kalich's twin, and a writer as well, but the fact that when Kalich finished the novel he had no idea whether it was a novel or a madman's ravings.

The Nihilesthete had gestated inside Kalich for five years before he finally worked up the courage to write it. He had not said a word to his twin or anybody else about it all those years until, finally, bursting at the seams, he went to a psychotherapist specializing in writer's block. After six sessions, Dr. Hatterer told him: Get out of here. You don't need me any longer. You're ready to write.

Kalich stood stock still. Perplexed.

Now that your brother has written and had his first novel published, you're ready to write your own. With twins it's always like that. Chicken and egg. First one. Then the other.

But which novel should he write, Kalich asked. He had another novel in him at the time.

The one deepest in you. The more important one.

That has to be *The Nihilesthete,* Kalich responded.

The lead character, Haberman, never leaves him. Seems as real to him as any actual person he's ever known.

The next day, Kalich went to his typewriter, an IBM Selectric II, and sat at his desk for thirty minutes. Two hours. Nothing... not a word came out.

The next day, the same thing. Not a word. Despite making every effort to wrench the words out of himself: nothing.

On the third day, Kalich tried something different. Rather than *The Nihilesthete,* Kalich decided to make an effort at his other novel, *The Zoo.* An Orwellian allegory taking place in the "Animal World." It poured out of him in thirty days. Single spaced. Hardly stopping. He was afraid to change his single spacing much less take a break for fear of losing it. All these years later and Kalich still looks upon the original manuscript with an almost obeisant humility as to what took place inside him. The mystery of—as he deemed it in a recent interview—the fecundity of the unconscious.

The Zoo was published that same year, followed two years later by the *The Nihilesthete*.

This is all said by way of introduction. For those early experiences laid the foundation for Kalich's evolving and ever-present concerns: The Mind-Body Split. And most importantly, the biographical narrative he is, hopefully, ready to write: *The Assisted Living Facility Library*, as well as the novel inside that book, *Mother Love*.

The gestation period for these two works has been eight years.

It always starts the same way: Kalich sees something. Or an image comes to him out of nowhere. In this case, a homeless woman lying prostrate on the ground at 58th Street and Fifth Avenue. A tattered rag blanket partially covering her emaciated frame. She shakes convulsively, possibly the aftermath of epileptic seizures. The woman is a ghastly sight. So much so, the various pedestrians hurrying by take no more than a cursory glance, and for many, even that is too much to bear. As for Kalich, he looks even closer. He can't help but notice the woman's gaze. Her eyes are riveted on a particular spot. The woman is gazing in the most extraordinary, loving way at a boy. No more than four to five years of age. The boy is nearly as forsaken and besotted as the woman. Yet, seems happy. Smiling. Giggling. And almost as extraordinary, the boy is returning the woman's gaze in the same loving way. They must be Mother and Son. That gaze, what the woman shares with the boy—Kalich has his next book.

Will he be equal to the task?

How much is left of him at this late date?

As his character, Haberman, did with the limbless artist, Brodski, in his novel, *The Nihilesthete*, Kalich returned the next day, and the next, to explore his find.

It was not difficult to coax Mother and the boy to reside with him. A daily diet of attention and smiles, several dollar bills and friendly touches, led the way. Kalich soon learned that Mother is a catatonic schizophrenic. She rarely, if ever, speaks. On those rare occasions, when she lifts herself from the ground to face the boy or attend to his needs, one notices how sometimes in midstream her body freezes, becomes fixed and locked as if arrested in limbo for a few seconds, sometimes more, until she moves on. No matter, within a week Kalich had won enough trust to invite Mother to take a shower at his apartment. Soon followed by a meal. Not only for Mother, but pancakes and eye-catching goodies for the boy.

It is good to have Mother and the boy in his apartment after all these years.

Sleeping alone is nothing.

Being alone is everything.

Not only will his character, Haberman, have welcome

guests to play his games with, but this Mother and boy filtered through his writer's prism is more than sufficient grist for his writer's mill.

What will Kalich do with them? The beauty and wonder are that it is entirely up to him. Mother and the boy will have only the smallest say in the matter.

At least Kalich thought so when he started his book's exploration.

But still, Kalich is old now. Not nearly the same person he was when he wrote *The Nihilesthete*. Actually, Kalich didn't really write *The Nihilesthete*. Every night, at about three, four in the morning, the novel would wake him, and images would race through his mind. Kalich had laid a notebook and pen at his bedside just to record those images. The next day, he would refine and edit them. But truly all the work, the genuinely creative and unknowable work, was done at night while asleep.

All Kalich did was take dictation.

With this book, it's very different for Kalich. He has something to say, but he can't say it very well. His body is tired; despite all the accumulated learning and books he's read, it's the body, the darkest and deepest regions that makes possible a writer's best work. If one can't mine that fecundity, call those powers forth, a writer is lost. All that's alive and vital originates in the body. And that's what Kalich wants to explore with Mother and the boy.

And especially in his character, Haberman.

OLD AGE

1. The phone never rings.
2. Fifty-seven out of Kalich's sixty-five friends, many close, have died.
3. Loss of desire, passion, lust.
4. To women—young or those still desirable—one is invisible.
5. Balance is gone. There is a chronic fear of falling.
6. Alone... all the time.
7. Television in the evening.
8. Arthritic hands—constantly dropping things: forks, knives, books, pens—everything.
9. Simone de Beauvoir was right: Old Age is a violation of human dignity.

Today, Kalich emptied out an entire section of The Great Russians. Dostoevsky and Tolstoy included. He never thought he could do that. Kalich laid aside Dostoevsky's *Notes from the Underground* and another of his favorites, Tolstoy's *The Death of Ivan Ilyich*—their fates to be decided later. As recompense, however, Kalich chose Pär Lagerkvist's *The Dwarf* as his first selection for his favorite one hundred to be taken to the Assisted Living Facility. He's always felt *The Dwarf* was the most interesting novel he's ever read on the nature of evil. And what makes the Swedish Nobel Prize winner even more special is that he also wrote *Pilgrim at Sea*, one of the most tender love stories Kalich has read. The Swedish master possessed the full range of the human spectrum.

At least when writing fiction.

When Kalich's novel, *The Nihilesthete,* was contracted to be published in Sweden, the publisher gave the novel to the country's leading semiotician for review. The semiotician called the publisher the following week to tell her that *The Nihilesthete* compared favorably to Lagerkvist's *The Dwarf*. Kalich considers that one of his greatest literary compliments, so much so that, when the publisher's farm suffered a prolonged drought and she had to cancel *The Nihilesthete*'s publication because of insufficient funds, rather than become despondent, Kalich helped finance the publication with his own money.

The country's leading semiotician's response to his book far outweighed any material or practical concerns.

To this day, Kalich speaks proudly of the experience.

If his body fails him and he cannot write, who is Kalich? How is he different than anyone else?

Than Mother?

Kalich's body has always been intact. Yet, he's found nothing more difficult than writing. So, it must be something else.

Something deeper.

Is it that different than love?

Kalich's two greatest capacities have always been to love

a woman and to write. Still, all his life he's dreaded writing and feared intimacy. He could not surrender himself to either. Imagine having someone to love and not being able to. What could be more punishing? Kalich experienced just that when already old, fifty-seven, he fell in love with The Young Harpist, Pia. Though The Harpist loved him in her way, at twenty, she could not reciprocate. Not with her body. Not physically.

For Kalich, it was a blessing and a curse.

Wouldn't it be interesting to explore Mother's love for the boy in just that way?

Happier days came with Sissie. The only woman who ever truly loved Kalich. He met her when he was forty. His habits were already set. Every day he would read ten pages or more from those books he considered most interesting in his library. Those pages, he often said, nourished him—not unlike a junkie who craves his fix. Walking out of the apartment one day, Sissie noticed how he would never leave without a book in his hand. Kalich explained his habit.

I'm like that too, Sissie said. Only with me, it's Mickford. I can't go anywhere without him. He's my security blanket.

At first Kalich thought it was lunacy to compare a dog to a book, but almost immediately he laughed it off. Book or dog, we all need something.

Back to *Mother Love*, Kalich's novel-in-progress. It never leaves him. And for that reason, he's grateful, even if Mother is not.

Haberman spent three hours playing with the boy. Laughing, smiling and feeding him, as well. Mother looked on from her space. What was she feeling, I wonder. Was she happy that the boy had such a caring friend? Or perhaps a little jealous of our time spent together? Impossible to tell at this early stage, but of one thing I'm certain: as the days and weeks proceed, Mother will reveal herself even if I won't. Not really.

Kalich still can't get into the rhythm of the work. It's not free flowing. Certainly nothing like his twin when he's at his Smith-Corona with the words just flooding out.

I'm going good, he exclaims. Nothing better.

Kalich has always experienced the opposite. A deep and penetrating sense of his mind and body not working together. A great divide between what he wants to say and his inability to write it. Even worse, he reflects. Not only has his literary culture been taken away and his library fast disappearing, but he's simultaneously losing who he is. Or was.

Himself.

Hard work and effort are of little use in times like these. Perseverance and tenacity are of no avail. Nor are all the books he's read and written. He's alone. Dying. Dead.

Still, he does have Mother and the boy.

Just prior to Dr. Hatterer advising him that he was ready to write, he strongly recommended that he leave Sissie. Sissie was manic depressive, and even though now on Lithium, and to an extent that helped, she would always be a burden. Not exactly what Kalich needed if he was to pursue his calling and write. Hearing the doctor's words, Kalich was relieved.

Though flattered for more than a year by Sissie's attentions, not to mention her physical beauty and larger-than-life (manic) personality and talents—Sissie was an artist—she could paint, sing, compose and was the most willing cook, a queen of the cuisine—Kalich never loved her. Respect, yes. Like, care for her, yes. But he never loved her as he did the Israeli when young and The Harpist when old.

His twin, as always, disagreed. Said he was crazy. He'll never do better. He was lucky to have her.

But Kalich knew what love was, and his brother just didn't.

In fairness, Kalich had been shaken one afternoon entering Sissie's apartment and seeing her standing in the middle of the room, arms twirling aloft like a gypsy dancer, blood dripping from her wrists and forearms down her naked body, all the while dancing a slow dance with glazed eyes and a beatific smile.

After Dr. Hatterer's recommendation, he left her. He never forgot the last words Sissie said to him at a restaurant when he told her he couldn't be with her any longer:

You should never have started with me if you couldn't finish.

She called him twenty-five years later. Told him she had loved him with all her heart. When he asked why. Why me?

Because you're an artist, she said.

He made up to call her for lunch as she was in New York for another week. But he knew it wasn't only lunch she wanted, and he never did.

This time his twin didn't say a word.

Today Haberman invited Mother for an early dinner. She had something to look forward to all day. Of course, Mother wasn't allowed to serve the generous portions to the boy. That beneficent act was reserved for Haberman alone.

And when dessert was served, chocolate pudding, the boy's favorite, Mother wasn't even permitted to watch. Only hear the boy slurping and smacking his lips with every mouthful. And for that reason, envision the boy's delight all the more.

As for Haberman—I literally spoon-fed the boy. After all, he is barely five years old...

Kalich spent the afternoon with one of the few friends he has left recently. A Yale School of Drama graduate in his late sixties touted along with John Guare, Sam

Shepherd, and Jean-Claude van Itallie, amongst a handful of other American playwrights, who were going to change theater. But when his opportunity came, and his debut production was unanimously panned by critics, he turned to fiction. Although capable of refined prose and well-crafted plotting, he really had nothing new or original to say, and despite several commercial publications, his career only met with a modicum of success. Ambition soon turned to tenacity, then to self-absorption. However, as his middle age quickly turned to getting old, he got lucky. He met a woman who was in a position to support him, and she gladly did so. He was able to sustain a moderately comfortable lifestyle. Two years ago, against all odds, he survived a colon cancer operation. Yet, through it all and with no real chance any longer at a breakthrough, or even making a mark, he continues to write.

Kalich asked his friend a question long overdue: Why?

It's the only time I feel alive was his friend's answer.

As his friend spoke those words, Kalich could hear the playwright's long-lost vitality return.

When *The Nihilesthete* was reviewed in Germany, one critic said Kalich was "mad" in the best sense of the word. Insane. Not shackled and chained by convention and the ordinary.

Still, to this day, Kalich reads his ten pages or more every morning when first awakening.

Why ten pages or more? He made himself a promise when graduating college that he would read ten pages or more of the greatest writers in the world every day of his life....

...And he's kept it. Except when writing his own books.

And he chronically continues to write, or at the very least, let gestate inside him his next book.

His next book—

For how long has Kalich been possessed by the idea that if he could call unto himself the demonic powers of his character, Haberman—

If he could bridge the chasm, which up to now has been confined and constrained to no more than pale words and abstract fictions—

That would vitalize and energize and free his own demonic power to live more than the life of the mind, the half-a-life he has known up to now.

Is this not precisely what Kalich wants to explore in his book *The Assisted Living Facility Library*, and the novel inside that book: *Mother Love*?

Each and every time Kalich walks on the street, or sits on a park bench, or enters a subway, he sees people, especially the young, reading their text messages or scanning their smartphones. Rarely, if ever, a book in their hand. On those rare occasions he does see a person reading a book, he can't help himself, and has to lean over the reader's shoulder to identify the title. Is it instinct? Reflex? A comrade-in-arms he is seeking? An old habit he can't let go? Or just idle curiosity?

Who can say?

An old friend, Adam Singer, formerly Arnie Singer, visited Kalich in New York. Kalich remembers him as the best-looking friend of his youth. Yet, he never pursued particularly attractive girls. He didn't want the aggravation. Over dinner he makes a comment Kalich would not have expected:

I've known you since City College days. More than fifty years. I still can't figure something out about you. You're always so upbeat. Positive. Always writing or working on a new project. Yet, you write the most depressing books.

Subject : I DON"T READ BECAUSE. . .
From: Adam@rr.com
Date: Tue, September 4, 2017 10:19 AM
To: Kalich@gmail.com

Dick:

"I DON'T READ BECAUSE WHEN I'M READING
I DON'T FEEL I'M DOING ANYTHING."

I didn't want to leave our last conversation without
clarifying my parting words.

We're different people. Ever since I've known you
you've wanted to do something great. Write the
great American novel. Be world famous. Win
awards. You're driven and I guess that's good
for you. It's who you are. I'm different. All I ever
wanted was to be happy. And that's hard enough.
I dont need anything more. Well, that's it. See you
next time   I'm in New York.

Love,
Adam

Feeling he'd dilly-dallied long enough, immediately after waking this morning, daily ablutions, and reading his ten pages, Kalich set about clearing his closet. The same week he moved into his apartment, he had a carpenter friend wall the entire space with bookshelves. Kalich has felt kindly towards the man ever since for having given him more than a generous price. At that time, Kalich could hardly have afforded more. The front section of the closet consists of seven showcase shelves, and on each side, creating a kind of horseshoe effect, are an additional fourteen shelves, one third the length of those shelves in the front. These shelves house his theater section and a major portion of South and Latin American novelists.

Kalich takes little time to choose from the American playwrights and selects for his favorite one hundred books the usual triad: Tennessee Williams's A *Streetcar Named Desire*; Arthur Miller's *The Crucible* and *Death of a Salesman*; and Eugene O'Neill's *The Iceman Cometh*. Hesitating for only a moment, he additionally selects Edward Albee's *Who's Afraid of Virginia Woolf?* That play alone earned him that status. And a little lat-

Kalich's Book Closet

er, he selects the Afro-American August Wilson's *Seven Guitars*. What Wilson did for his time and people is no less than what Chekhov did for turn-of-the-century Russia. It doesn't take him much longer to choose from his European collection. Chekhov's *The Seagull* and *The Cherry Orchard*, followed closely by Ionesco's *Exit the King* and Beckett's *Waiting for Godot*.

Of course, Samuel Beckett holds a special place for Kalich. His *Waiting for Godot* stands alone in depicting the human predicament in the second half of the twentieth century. In fact, Kalich has placed Beckett's entire oeuvre on a single top shelf in his living room area. Adjacent to that shelf are Joyce, Márquez, Georges Perec, and Fernando Pessoa.

The Latin-American novelists cost Kalich the better part of the afternoon. The largesses from this continent are so vast and vital, so different from his kindred Europeans, especially Eastern-Europeans, that Kalich is not embarrassed to admit that he has always been intimidated by such writers as the Tolstoyan-size Gabriel García Márquez; as well as the wit, wisdom and levity of José Saramago. But in an inexplicable move, even to himself, he selects for his favorite bookshelf the far lesser known Ivan Ângelo's *The Celebration*. Kalich was young and still searching for his voice when he first came upon this book. Needless to say, the Brazilian's bold invention combined with the way he played with time and space made a lasting impression on the young writer.

But still, hidden away behind the showcase volumes are hundreds more volumes and, after availing himself of a three-step ladder, he parses through their worth and value. After another two hours Kalich finds his energy ebbing; the effort has taken its toll. Stamina, strength, mobility have deserted him in recent years and he's forced to take a break. His balance, as all the rest of him, is not what it used to be. The three-step ladder costs him as much as it gives. Additionally, he has to deal with dead insects and paper; bits and pieces of paper. Paper ripped, torn, frayed, yellowed and dog-eared. Pages of paper have shed themselves one way or another from the books, as well as dust, dustballs, and sundry paperclips. And despite stops and starts, after another hour Kalich is completely worn out. But no, he won't quit. He can't. He perseveres and between more stops and starts, deep breaths and stretching both his arms and legs, another 150 books make their way to the trash pile. Kalich has always been megalomaniacally stubborn when it comes to his books. And his work is not yet done. Taking the shortest time to rest, he plods on. But this time rather than deciding the fate of each book individually, book by book, if not page by page, he allows whole sections, entire bookshelves to plummet to the floor. Such a tactic stands him in good stead, and by day's end he's not only lessened his count by 750 to 1,000 books, he's additionally found another two books to take with him to the Assisted Living Facility.

Simone de Beauvoir's *The Second Sex,* and her Parisian compatriot Violette Le Duc's *La Bâtarde*; or as her peers and colleagues affectionately labelled her: The Ugly Woman of France.

But that night Kalich can't sleep. With so many books he so carelessly let fall from the closet shelves to the floor, he feels it is he who is homeless, not Mother. And the next morning, like a guilt-ridden soldier who neglected his duty, he returns to the killing fields to give each and every book their rightful due. Fortunately, a lifetime's habit of paper-clipping especial pages makes his task easier. His past labors do not go unrewarded. And to his surprise (Kalich has been an elitist all his life; only one of his many failings, and strengths) he selects Erica Jong's blockbuster *Fear of Flying* as a worthy candidate for his favorite 100 bookshelf. The visceral flesh and blood immediacy of Jong's book makes up for her weaknesses.

Whether at the Dentist's office or accidentally meeting a neighbor in Central Park on a bench.

Train.

Ticket line.

On the street.

Or in the midst of a bowel movement at home.

Whether attending a lecture at the 92nd Street Y or on the lifecycle machine at Equinox for his arthritic hips.

Watching TV

Ball game

Movie or

    or

Just waiting for the red light to turn green.

Has there ever been a day in Kalich's life when he didn't have a book in his hand or his eye on a page?

There's no difference between a writer and anyone else; it's just a matter of what a person invests his time and effort in.

Those words were spoken to Kalich by a young woman, Maren, at the end of a date in front of her Brooklyn home. Kalich did not respond. To reduce a writer to an algorithm of time and effort, rather than architectural wonder, or even divine ordinance, begged credulity.

Before Kalich left a short time later, the young woman asked him what he thought of marriage and family. This time Kalich didn't mince words.

If you feel that way, the young woman said, what will you do when you're old?

I'll worry about that when I'm old, Kalich responded.

Kalich never forgot the young woman's words.

Kalich was twenty years old.

What makes you think being a writer and writing is the only way to spend your life?

Those words were spoken to Kalich by Robbie Phillips, a plastics manufacturer from New Jersey, while dining at Abe's restaurant. Abe later explained that Robbie was upset, as his son had chosen to go abroad to study philosophy, rather than join his firm.

Kalich never forgot the plastic manufacturer's words, either.

Kalich was forty years old.

Kalich also remembers that the young woman's father was a Catskill Mountains comic.

He remembers that because his parents vacationed every summer for four to eight weeks at the hotel Klein's Hillside, in Parksville, NY.

It is only fair to assume his parents took the twins with them. Especially since Kalich has always described those summers at the hotel as paradisiacal.

Nor is it farfetched to assume that Maren's father performed at the hotel's nightclub, where he made a lasting impression on the young Kalich.

An impression good or bad.

Presumably good.

Klein's Hillside was known for basketball—in those years, a good deal of the staff were college players with always one or two college All-Americans sprinkled amongst them. However, the real coup was having NBA and Eastern League players such as Nat Militzok of the NY Knicks and Eddie Younger of the Scranton Miners perform as well. One summer, Kalich recalls the NBA's first great Big Man, George Mikan, being on staff. Since his parent's bungalow was next to the Mikans', the eleven-year-old Kalich and his twin got to know George Mikan well. He remembers him as a gentle giant, warm and kind, with a quick smile and thick glasses; his wife, Pat, was pregnant at the time with Larry, who would eventually go on to be an NBA player.

Still, Kalich's fondest memory of the hotel was the Chinese cookies, cold milk and chocolate syrup served from a small white pitcher by the matronly Minnie in the children's dining room, which Kalich and his brother visited without fail every day at 3 p.m. There were always one or two basketball players there as well.

Twelve-year-old Kalich with George Mikan

Evidently, they loved the cookies and milk almost as much as the twins.

Then there was a water fight with the seventeen-year-old boat boy, Rudy, who was also on the basketball team. Even at that young age, Kalich could recognize Rudy's special gift. When playing softball and tossing the ball in from the outfield, he threw the ball faster and with more force and life than Kalich had seen anyone do before.

(Rudy Hernandez went on to become the first player of Dominican descent to pitch in the Major Leagues.)

But mostly, Kalich loved playing third base in the softball games with the other guests and staff. Gifted himself at that age as a fielder, and always chosen to participate, he felt he could field any ball hit to him. And for the most part, he did. It was the first time Kalich felt he possessed anything approaching a consummate skill.

He has never quite realized that feeling of excellence since.

Certainly not in his writing.

And, of course, how could he forget? There was the

busboy Elliot, only three years older than Kalich at the time, 19, who had all the pretty girls at the hotel flocking around his table morning, noon, and night. Whether it was his good looks, smile or just sheer charm, Kalich didn't know. But he did know, or at least said to himself and his brother—I'll be just like Elliot in a few years.

Was it, Kafka, who said: Youth is the time to dream?

Kalich credits those paradisiacal years for giving him sufficient faith and trust to withstand all the cumulative hardships and disappointments he has had to endure later in life. Of course, the greatest part of this ballast, as he would be the first to acknowledge, originated in the unconditional love he received from his mother (his mother told all who would listen, including the twins many times over, that she prayed to have twins) and in the unbreakable bond he shares with his brother.

If it's true that the higher one climbs, the greater the fall, then it also might be true and serve as an explanation as to why Kalich was able to reach such highs and plummet to such depths both in his writing and personal life.

However, please be aware of the theologian Abraham Heschel's maxim: Simple minds come up with simple solutions.

But of course, Kalich has never been accused of being simple....

...Except by his twin brother.

At eighteen, his father, the cantor, obtained for Kalich a position at the famed hotel, Kutcher's Country Club, in Monticello, NY. Like Klein's Hillside, Kutcher's was also known for basketball, having given the sixteen-year-old phenom, Wilt Chamberlain, a job as a bellhop.

Kalich started as a boat boy, but when a woman fell in a boat and broke her collarbone, the owner, Milton Kutcher, called Kalich into his office.

What happened? he asked.

Kalich's answer was, if nothing else, forthright: The woman was on the dock and, as he was in the midst of reading a concluding page of a chapter in Tolstoy's *War and Peace,* he asked her to wait a minute. And she didn't.

Oh, that explains it, said the always wise and under-standing owner.

Kalich was reassigned to the dining room as a busboy, where he promptly dropped two trays, one purposefully on an all-too-nagging female guest.

He finished the last six weeks of the summer as a children's counsellor, where he was able to catch up on his summer reading list: Dostoevsky's *The Brothers Karamazov, The Idiot,* and *The Friend of the Family.* And Thomas Mann's *The Magic Mountain* and *Confessions of Felix Krull, Confidence Man.* Though Dostoevsky and Mann are known for their epochal psycho-philosophical novels (and rightly so) both writers possessed the full range, a comic genius, and Kalich quickly fell under their comedic spell. In *The Friend of the Family,* Foma Fomitch, a failed writer placed in a bourgeois home as mentor to the children, takes out his impotent rages from top to bottom, on servants and children, the matriarch and patriarch, as a pedagogical tyrant. Kalich saw himself and a thousand others in Foma in our contemporary world. As for Felix Krull, the blue-eyed bronze-skinned pageboy who incarnates vertical mobility; who realizes every male (and female) phantasy; who mixes, hobnobs, manipulates and exploits from the lowest rung to the top tier of European society; Kalich understands him as a precursor to our own contemporary culture, which blurs distinctions between phantasy and reality: where everything is possible because there is no substantive and coherent reality to begin with.

How positive was Kalich's response to these two books? Visit Kalich's Facility and you'll find both, Dostoevsky's *The Friend of the Family* and Mann's *Confessions of Felix Krull, Confidence Man,* in their library.

Additionally, Kalich had a heated sexual affair with a Riverdale housewife, whose husband stayed in New York Monday through Friday to work, and, at the least, she was freed during the week from playing house. All in all, it was a memorable summer for young Kalich.

YOU LIVE SUCH A FUCKING SMALL LIFE—
IT'S RIDICULOUS!

His twin's barrage came with a phone call early in the morning:

Do you know the company Samsung?

No, Kalich answered hesitatingly; already anticipating all that would follow:

No. Of course not. You know nothing except your books. My Knute at sixteen knows more about the real world than you. Samsung is one of South Korea's largest companies. And it's just been announced that their government has sentenced its CEO to prison for five years.

So, what do I care? I'm a writer. I've never read a single page of the Wall Street Journal, either.

That's your problem.

You never go anywhere.

Never been married.

Have no children.

Never travel.

Never go out to dinner with friends. With Anyone.

You never do anything.

You live HALF-A-LIFE!

Even if his brother was projecting his own frustrations and failures onto him, as he well knew, it still hurt. The sheer accumulation of criticism and sustaining ambivalence of his twin had become almost impossible to endure.

Ever since Pia, you've become worse than ever, and he hung up.

Where his ideas come from, Haberman doesn't know. But he does know if he executes them well, he will be rewarded. He races into Mother's tiny space.

"Mother!" he exclaims, "Something's come up. I have to leave. I don't know for how long or even when I'll be back. Possibly after the weekend. You'll have to care for our boy the rest of the week and through the weekend, at least. But don't worry. I left enough food in the fridge to feed an army. And you have my cellphone number. You can always call me if a problem comes up."

(Haberman is confident Mother will not try to escape. Not only has she no place to go, she has little means to get there.)

Imagine Mother's disappointment when Haberman returned, not Sunday night or Monday morning, but early the next day. The majority of those precious hours Mother wasted sleeping.

"I'm so sorry, Mother, it was a false alarm. Once I learned my business affairs were in order, I was so anxious to return to the boy, I couldn't even spare a moment to call and let you know."

Mother cannot hide her feelings. The comic-tragic way her shoulders sagged, and her face dropped, especially for a catatonic for whom any movement, no matter how small, must be Promethean, sustained Haberman for at least the remainder of the week.

Although Kalich spent his mature years writing about the literary culture's demise and how the image has usurped the word, on another level, a deeper level, he never thought it would happen so quickly during his lifetime.

Indeed, once finishing *The Nihilesthete* and "seeing" his next novel, then titled *Transfiguration of the Commonplace*, he began telling friends and peers that:

Words have become the enemy of writers.

Those he told scoffed and smiled, but Kalich knew what he knew and after allowing the novel to gestate for another twenty-five years, he finally found the courage to write it.

Even if the title (now called *Penthouse F*) and form changed radically from his original version, the content (and this Kalich finds remarkable) remained the same.

three

the mcdonaldization of the literary marketplace

Authors don't write solely from within disparate literary histories. They also write from within disparate economic ecologies. Despite the Romantic myths to the contrary, nobody ever sits down to compose in an ahistorical vacuum outside the marketplace.

A quick history lesson concerning that marketplace over the course of the last century or so. During the sixties, more than 100 publishing houses thrived in Manhattan. The seventies saw a major oil crisis and recession that resulted in a movement toward consolidation and commodification in the book industry—toward maximizing profits and minimizing risk. By the eighties, there were only 79 publishers left in Manhattan. By the nineties, 15.

Currently, there are only five that bring out fiction: HarperCollins, the Penguin Group, Random House, Simon & Schuster, and Time Warner. Only five, and yet they are responsible for 80 percent of the bestsellers out there. Combine them with the next five, and that figure rises to 98 percent. Most of the Big Five are subsidiaries of vast entertainment corporations (Random House, for instance, of Bertelsmann; HarperCollins of News Corporation), which in good part use those book outlets as tax write-offs.

Although it surely is not the case that the Big Five don't bring out some exciting innovative fiction (Mark Z. Danielewski, Lydia Davis, Mario Vargas Llosa, Thomas Pynchon, and J. M. Coetzee rush to mind), it is the case that the trend in commercial publishing over the last half century has been toward a narrower, safer, blander vision of writing driven by corporate authors like Anne Rice, Stieg Larsson, Stephen King, Dan Brown, and David Sedaris, not to mention the young ones publishers perceive and sell as The Next Hot Thing.

Why Is It So Goddamned Hard to Make a Living as a Writer Today?

By Douglas Preston

Doug Preston was the keynote speaker at the inaugural New Mexico Writers Dinner at La Fonda Hotel in Santa Fe on March 2nd. We reprint his remarks here with his permission and our thanks.

I have no doubt that almost all of you in this room struggle with a central question in your lives: Why is it so goddamned hard to make a living as a writer today?

A recent study by the Authors Guild showed that from 2009 to 2015, the average income of a full-time author decreased 30 percent, from $25,000 a year to $17,500 a year. For part-time authors, the average income decreased 38 percent, from $7,250 a year to $4,500. Full-time authors with more than 25 years of experience saw the greatest drop—a 67 percent decrease from $28,750 to $9,500.

The collapse of authors' incomes is not a problem. It's not even a crisis. It's a catastrophe. And not just for us, but for our nation as a whole. Writing is the lifeblood of American culture, of democracy, and of freedom. It is under assault as never before in the history of the Republic.

The work starts when you finish the book, novel, screenplay, play.

How many times has Kalich said this to his twin brother over a lifetime? Once his brother finished a first draft he would give it to Kalich, and he, "The Good Twin," would assume the role of editor. More often than not, laboring for as many as three hours on a butchered page. Though a larger talent than Kalich, a natural writer, his twin would never pay attention to details, master the craft. And what else is writing but craft and detail? Still, when "going good" as he deems it, he could spend five, ten, as many as twelve hours a day at his Smith-Corona. As for Kalich, an hour or two a day and he's content.

For Kalich, writing has always been as much about self-overcoming as talent or inspiration.

Even before his twin became a major college basketball handicapper, he would not lift a finger to help the cause. Never make a phone call or take a meeting. The business side of writing he consigned entirely to Kalich. Finding an agent, publisher, editor, development exec, producer, someone, anyone, who could open a door, help move the property, has always been Kalich's responsibility and domain. His twin would never put himself on the line. Was never able to ask, only tell. He could never be anything but the Big Man. To get on the phone as an anonymous caller, speak to an unknown person in a position of authority, was just something he wouldn't, couldn't do. Nowhere is this more evident than when socializing. At a party at his Central Park South apartment, boasting the most magnificent terrace overlooking the park, he's all charm and bombast, a master of small talk, running to and fro, from guest to friend. But if he's asked to attend a gathering where he's just another face in the crowd, a member of the chorus, anonymous—he won't go. It's not simply grandiosity, egoism, or some hybrid psychological malady. No, Kalich believes the problem is ontological. What one twin is, the other is not. A particular form of Being and Non-being.

The twins' mother said as much when they were but five or six. Your brother, she said, will always have to be the Big Man. You... you won't. You won't need anybody or anything. You'll always be sufficient unto yourself.

Kalich has always thought that his brother's opposite-side-of-the-coin self took root when they were eight to ten years of age. Being the more gifted at sports, Kalich was always chosen first by the other kids to play punchball, stickball, curb ball. His brother, rarely chosen, if at all. Countless times after making an error or striking out, Kalich remembers his twin running home with clenched fists and contorted mouth, holding back tears. What he did upstairs in the twins' room, Kalich didn't give much thought to at the time. He was too young. But now he believes that's where it all started. That it's part and parcel of being a twin.

Perhaps the biggest part.

Kalich notices that in the course of creating this draft of his novel, *Mother Love*, he has occasionally written "I" or "Kalich" rather than "Haberman" when referring to his character. At first, he was upset with himself and made the necessary corrections. But now he understands this to be a good thing. Among other concerns, his novel is about the blurring of distinctions between fiction and reality, and if he, the author, is confused, is caught betwixt and between, he can only imagine how confusing it must be to the reader.

After finishing the final draft of his novel, *The Nihilesthete,* on April 25, 1981, Kalich immediately set to work finding a publisher. He wrote letters, made phone calls, met with editors, agents, publishers (from small houses) and could be seen daily carrying padded bags containing his manuscript on his way to the post office. The submissions were plentiful, the rejection letters that followed, equally so. By the second year, Kalich had received no less than twenty-eight rejection letters. He was so despairing, his strength ebbed, his spirit flagged, he lost faith and trust in himself, as well as his work; and perhaps worst of all, the novel that had been inside him since he had completed *The Nihilesthete, Transfiguration of the Commonplace,* was not being written. As he often told his twin:

I'm so depressed, I can't even lift a pen.

Yet, he continued to make every effort to find a publisher for *The Nihilesthete* and realize his life-long ambition to have at least one novel that belonged on the shelf with other worthy writers.

Kalich learned much during these years. He was in the habit of saving every rejection letter—a sort of way to memorialize and give evidential credence to his life. Doing so, he came to understand that the letters were all of the same tenor. Either the readers loved the book or hated it. There was no in between. Gradually, it came to him that editors and readers were no different than anybody else. They were not assessing the novel for its individual literary merit, or lack thereof; by any time-tested critical criteria, but rather by something deeper, more inward, personal. It was more like an inkblot test, the Rorschach: each and every reader, whether positive or negative, was receiving from the novel what he or she brought to it. It was that simple, no more, no less. Some could handle the novel, others could not. The response was close to equal. Half liked it, half did not. But all concerned voiced a definitive opinion. Those that did not like it said: Unreadable, painful, perverse, unbearable. How could you expect to find a publisher for a novel like this? Why'd you write it—to win a literary award? The other half, those whose temperaments and natures allowed them to assimilate, integrate, be open to Kalich's demonic vision, were inordinately positive. Several likened him to Kafka. One senior editor at Harper and Row, Ted Solotaroff, compared the book to the Hungarian novelist George Konrad's *The Case Worker*, going so far as to say, *The Nihilesthete* starts where *The Case Worker* ended.

Even Samuel Beckett, the absolute standard bearer of great writers in the second half of the 20th century (and Kalich's own favorite), was mentioned. But despite this, no publication was offered.

Sorry, but the present marketplace cannot support a book such as yours.

Drenke Villen, the venerable editor at Harcourt Brace, who had published so many of Kalich's favorite European authors, broke his heart when, after keeping the book for six months, she finally wrote him a letter: In my heart of hearts, I truly wanted to publish this book, but I just could not find others here to support me.

In the fifth year, after seventy-four rejections, his twin visited him late one night at his apartment.

Forget getting your novel published, he said. It's not going to happen. We can go into business. We're as well connected in this city as anyone. If we put half as much effort into business as we have into writing novels, we can have a good and successful life.

No, said Kalich. There's one publisher left. If he rejects it, then all right. But he wanted, needed, to take this one last shot.

On March 30, 1986, the seventy-fifth publisher, Permanent Press of Sag Harbor, NY, Marty and Judy Shepherd, said yes.

Kalich at his desk, working on The Nihilesthete

THE DIAL PRESS
1 Dag Hammarskjold Plaza
245 EAST 47 STREET • NEW YORK, N.Y. 10017
Tel. (212) 832-7300
Cable Address: DIALPUBS

TELEX: 238781 DELL

August 2, 1982

Richard Kalich
65 Central Park West
Penthouse F
New York, NY 10023

Dear Mr. Kalich:

    This is quite a tour-de-force and I'm sure it will suit
someone absolutely perfectly. But I really didn't like it,
its artistry aside -- it's quite distressing (the narrator,
that is), and while that quality might be put to good use in
the theater, I don't think it's redeemed in the manuscript.
Anyway, thanks for letting us have a chance at the book.

                    Yours sincerely,

                    Frau McCullough

                    Mrs. Frances McCullough
                    Senior Editor

64

W · W · NORTON & COMPANY · NEW YORK · LONDON

500 FIFTH AVENUE · NEW YORK 10110 · CABLES: SEAGULL/NEW YORK · TELEX 12-7634 · TEL. (212) 354-5500

December 17, 1982

Mr. Dick Kalich
The Kalich Organization
65 Central Park West
Penthouse F
New York, N. Y. 10023

Dear Mr. Kalich:

I'm afraid the battle here is lost. I won't go into great detail but the decision not to make an offer was based on a feeling that what your book asks the reader to undergo is not repaid in a credible meaning or insight. There is a good deal of both, but in the end not enough to which the normal human can relate.

For example, at the end the feeling is that Haberman is quite mad mad in a way that really does not tell a not-mad reader anything about himself or his world, and Brodsky is a human with an un-believable I. Q. of 18, again not a person with whom one can feel a kinship.

Without a reward of the sort I am groping for, the course the reader must run is just too rough.

We may well be wrong. I, personally, would like to see your book published and hope you will find a publisher to prove us wrong.

Sincerely,

Eric P. Swenson

EPS:ec

enc. - by messenger

P. S. I am sending you an extra copy of the manuscript which we had made in order to speed up readings (!).

65

The Vanguard Press · 424 MADISON AVENUE · NEW YORK, N. Y. 10017

TELEPHONE: PLAZA 3-3906   CABLE ADDRESS: VANGPRESS

3/8/83

Mr. Richard Kalich
65 Central Park West (Penthouse F)
New York, N.Y. 10023

Dear Mr. Kalich:

I am sorry the final decision here was not to make
an offer of publication of NIHILESTHETE. As others
have said, the novel is an unforgetable, extraordinary
work, painful and often terrifying, but my associates
are not of that opinion, and so I have to agree the
answer now is no. Like Miss Garthe, I wonder how you
were able to live through writing it, for it must have
been painful for you, too.

The manuscript is being returned herewith, with our
thanks for your thought of us and with the hope NIHIL-
ESTHETE will find an enthusiastic welcome elsewhere
soon. All good wishes from

                          Sincerely,

                          Evelyn Shrifte

                          Evelyn Shrifte

es/e/enc.

66

Dick Kalich
65 Central Park West
New York, New York
10023

April 25, 1985

Dear Mr. Kalich,

I'm returning enclosed THE NIHILESTHETE which I have
been holding on to for much too long.

You are correct, this is off the wall. I read it and
a reader read it. Though we did not agree on everything,
we both thought that after the initial interest and un-
folding of the heinous Haberman's plot, it became slow
and unrelenting. I didn't see any major problems with
the writing; in most parts it was competent and sure-
handed. I would have liked to see a little more dazzle
overall, though I understand that your style is part
of the effect you are trying to create.

Besides your subject, I really don't see that there
is anything here that makes the book stand out enough
to publish it as a first novel. Although you probably
abhor suggestions at this point, I would point out
that the problem seems to be with Haberman. Sure, he
is bereft of all morality and decency. Still, whatever
is motivating him does not come across as strongly as
it should, answering the reader's emphatic 'why?'.

I thank you for sending this along and being patient.

Yours,

Michael Sanders

Simon & Schuster Building
1230 Avenue of the Americas
New York, NY 10020
212 246-2121
Published by Pocket Books
A Division of Simon & Schuster

One year later, *The Nihilesthete* was published. The first two reviews by the trade publications, *Kirkus* and *Publishers Weekly*, bombed the book mercilessly. Evidently, the reviewers, like so many before them, couldn't tolerate the book's bleak vision. Once again, Kalich met his brother. Once again, only this time more assertively, his twin argued that they should enter the business world.

No, Kalich said again, Not yet.

He had read a book review in *The New York Times* two or three years ago. The review was brilliant. It's stayed with him all these years. He wanted to try to send the novel to that reviewer.

George Stade, novelist, book critic, ex-football player, Irish tough, and head of Columbia University's Comparative Literature Department, called Kalich back the same week.

I have enough nightmares of my own, he said, I didn't need to add to them by reading your book. But I want you to know: *Nihilesthete* is a masterpiece. I'll do all I can to help.

From that time on, *The Nihilesthete* went on to collect more than seventy-five superlative reviews throughout the world. As well as find twelve international publications.

Kalich was fifty years old when *The Nihilesthete* was published.

When Kalich read in *The New York Times* that their chief book reviewer, who spent the last 28 years with the Gray Lady, was among those who took the money and ran...

...his first thought was:

Michiko Kakutani was Kalich's neighbor for most of those years, and despite repeated requests on his part, and his brother's (admittedly, the requests became increasingly aggressive as the years passed), to review his novels, she never did. But more to the point, and what he wants all to know, is that this *New York Times* book reviewer who held so much power, who could make a career with a stroke of her pen, figuratively speaking, would, each and every time they met on the elevator, stand in a corner, facing the wall like a naughty five-year-old, and not make a sound for the duration.

And for those who don't believe Kalich, his address at the time was 65 Central Park West, NYC, 10023.

The Nihilesthete by Richard Kalich
(Permanent: $17.95; 155 pp.)

Reviewed by Stewart Lindh

"The Nihilesthete" contains two dimensions—one is the grimy, opaque descent into the hell of Harlem and the dismal odyssey of a demented social worker's attempts to destroy one of his cases: a cri du chat. The second dimension is parabolic: A symbol of negation tries to eradicate all light in a soul and, in doing so, creates in the midst of a physical midnight a human sunrise.

The novel is disturbing and, like a tiny Tar Baby encountered on the shelf of existence, cannot be put down once contact is made. In the tradition of "Notes From the Underground," "The Metamorphosis" and "The Case Worker," Richard Kalich's first novel is the manifestation of an unhappy consciousness finding an objective correlative in the world and then wrapping itself around the object, to fester the form into submission.

Like the Chinese artist who escaped death at the hands of the emperor by fleeing aboard a boat he painted into one of his seascapes, Brodski eludes Haberman by ricocheting off the world into his own cosmos, to paint forever.

Haberman forgot what Wallace Stevens reminds us in "The Well Dressed Man With a Beard":

After the final no there comes a yes

And on that yes the future world depends.

"The Nihilesthete" is a journey into the encyclopedia of lost souls. It is a brilliant, hammer-hitting, lights-out novel.

The cri du chat is a cri du coeur.

Lindh is editing "The Theory of Sand," a novel based on his adventures in Saudi Arabia.

A Cross-Hatching of Private Hells

THE NIHILESTHETE
By Richard Kalich
Permanent Press, $17.95, 155 pages

REVIEWED BY DAVID BALLARD

Completely demented from start to finish, Richard Kalich's first novel, "The Nihilesthete" is nevertheless one of the most powerfully written books of this decade. Subtitled "Case Record of Robert Haberman. Caseworker" the book recounts in vivid detail the bizarre relationship between Haberman and a man who could easily win the best character of the year award, if there were such a thing. Brodski.

Haberman's extreme and morbid fascination with Brodski would be a little hard to swallow were it not for the author's excellent portrayal of the caseworker as a complete case himself. Shortly before his first visit to Brodski's house, Haberman describes in manic fashion the delicious agony he feels every day of his lonely life, especially on the weekend: "Nothing is more difficult than the weekend. Television can take us so far, the telephone never rings, and one can manage just so many trips

It is to Kalich's utter credit as an author that he has created such an unforgettable pairing as Brodski and Haberman. His real genius is a writer, though, is in the way he allows their relationship to evolve and drive the story forward to its conclusion, keeping the use of conventional plot devices to a minimum. The simplicity and uncanny grace of Kalich's prose becomes even more apparent once Haberman has gathered all the paints, brushes and brushes

ence and twisted logic. If Kalich meant his two characters to be condensed versions of the unwashed masses of New York City and what subculture for enlightened government in our time, then it's not hard to imagine the incredible inhumanity that Kalich lays word by gut-wrenching word across the pages of "The Nihilesthete." But one is never sure who is the greater victim.

Kalich's attacks on the bastions of rationality (public health departments and the city employees who run them) within the confines of what is essentially a two-character book, are as accurate and as poignant as those made by Ken Kesey in his much broader "One Flew Over the Cuckoo's Nest." And Kalich's ren-

Kakutani, Risen among 100 NY Times buyouts

MEDIA INK

By KEITH J. KELLY

MICHIKO Kakutani, the chief book reviewer for the New York Times, who spent 38 years at the Gray Lady, was among those who took the money and ran as part of the recently completed buyout program at the paper.

Pulitzer Prize-winning reporter **James Risen** also took the buyout.

It is believed that when the dust settles, about 100 employees will have departed — some with more than a little arm-twisting.

Of the 76 NewsGuild members who applied for a buyout, 72 had been accepted by Thursday, according to Guild President **Grant Glickson**.

At least 16 nonunion members were said to have taken the deal.

News about Kakutani's departure came the same day as the Times issued a generally favorable quarterly earnings report. In its results, the Times revealed that booming digital subscriptions passed the 2 million paid mark and its digital subscription revenue passed the slumping print ad revenue figure for the first time.

Overall revenue in the quarter was $407 million, up 9 percent from a year ago. Adjusted operating income was $67.1 million, up 23 percent.

Most of the those exiting are from the copy desk, which is being wiped out and replaced by a new brand of uber editor who will work on print, digital and video.

In all, 100 copy editors were told their jobs were goners — although a good number landed some of the 65 new super-editor jobs.

Times CEO **Mark Thompson** said in his talk to analysts, "Our newsroom is undergoing a process to streamline its operation to match our ambitions for digital journalism and free up resources to put more journalistic boots on the ground to deliver more investigations and help us further develop our capabilities in visual journalism."

Said one insider who survived:

"The mood is grim acceptance. But also exasperation, that when the Times is putting up great numbers, it has chosen to undermine the product by eliminating the free-standing copy desk."

Today, when Kalich is asked what his best book is (he's written four novels to date), he always answers the same: He doesn't know which novel is his best, but he knows which one cost him the most: *The Nihilesthete*.

But why? How could that be? Of all your books, *The Nihilesthete* received more acclaim and artistic success than any of your others. Yes, that may well be true, Kalich answers. But what a book costs a writer cannot be measured in such simplistic terms as success or failure. Fame or fortune. The only true measure is that despite all the acclaim and affirmation, he still wasn't able to write his next novel for another twenty-one years.

In spite of being raised in a Jewish Orthodox home and having a renowned cantor for a father, Kalich never believed in God. Instead, he believed in The Word.

Not so different than the rabbi who preached Moshiach is coming to his flock.

Indeed, well into his fifties when his first published novel was making its way into the world, Kalich still believed The Word could redeem the world.

He also believed in Transcendence. No longer. Not now. Now that the literary culture is so over, as one playwright put it only last season in a play that had a short run, and with his books so fast disappearing from his bookshelves, and by his own hand yet, Kalich no longer believes.

Kalich's lifelong appreciation of beauty has begun to fade, too.

In past years, Kalich's habit was to fill his toothbrush rack with different colored brushes. The same with his liquid detergents. Each of the six selected for the particular aesthetic value of their color and design. Each blending harmoniously with the other like a painter designs his palette. No artist could have been more scrupulous selecting his paints. Even on Sundays, when he habitually takes his daily stroll in Central Park, sits on his favorite bench on 59th Street off Central Park South to read a book, or just observe the Sunday crowd, he never fails to peer across the lake where the great white bird sits still as a statue perched on its tree branch.

Yes, beauty has nourished Kalich all his life: the face, grace and lissome figure of a young woman; the laughter, smile and voice of a child; even an ancient homeless mariner, lying prostrate on the ground: Kalich has always surrendered himself to beauty. Has always been able to find beauty in every nook and cranny. But no longer. Not now.

Now, since the literary culture is so over, and his books are so fast vanishing before his own eyes, Kalich suffers from a profound Absence of Beauty in his life.

It is not enough to say that Kalich's books are fast disappearing from his bookshelves. Not only those books he selects for his favorite bookshelf, but each and every book in his library has had a life (now death) prior to being tossed into the trash pile. Kalich has created a Book of Quotes, assembling from his books' encyclopedic pages those passages he never wanted to lose or forget. Also, he has a separate folder of Book Titles, for all those volumes he has read over the years. Not only titles, but the precise date and time he finished reading the book. And that is not to mention how with red, blue and green colored pencils, he has underlined those sentences and paragraphs he just couldn't let go of at the time of reading them. Nor how he's written inside the pages as well as the blank end pages of the books a wealth of anecdotal notes, ideas and thoughts catalyzed by his reading. For that reason, the trashed books have little material value and cannot be sold to any bookstore nor dealer. Neither Strand Bookstore or Charlie on West 68th Street. Other than by Kalich, and sometimes not even by him, these books can no longer be deciphered, much less read by any future readers.

It goes without saying that there are gems amongst them.

Charlie—West 68th Street and Columbus Avenue

Kalich awakes in the middle of the night terrified that his mind will go blank. That he has nothing more to say. That what he has already said has no value. His book is not made up of the trappings of a novel. Lacks continuity, coherence. So many doubts seep into his mind. Is it a novel he is writing? Does what he is writing make sense? To the reader? To himself? Is it really what he wants to say? Can he say it? Is he equal to the task?

But at this wizened age of his life, he knows all this is to be expected. That it is a good thing. It means he is not writing a novel he can write, but the novel he can hardly imagine.

Kalich is certain other scribes have felt the same.

Those who either know Kalich personally or from his earlier books, know that Kalich has experienced two great loves in his life. Once when young, the other when old.

The first was with the Israeli, Hana. A Holocaust survivor, passed around from soldier to soldier as a tot, somehow reuniting with her parents in Israel and growing up on a kibbutz. By the time Kalich met her in July 1961, in New York, she was already the mother of two small children, Sheba, 8, and Harvey, 5. After making love to Harvey's mother, Kalich would go into his room and watch the child's face as he slept and hold his little thumb. It always seemed to Kalich that though fast asleep, by reaching out to him, the little fellow was grounding himself to the world. Hana, described by all who saw her as not one of the most, but the most beautiful woman they ever saw, was the mistress of one of the more powerful and charismatic men in New York. Where does she get the strength? Abe would say on the phone to him. I fucked her like a horse yesterday afternoon and then last night she goes to you.

Kalich could only laugh. And agree. If one just touched Hana's elbow she would have an orgasm. At twenty-four he knew that much, but not much more. But though it was a deep love, a once-in-a-lifetime love, the romance was short-lived. Two summer months and then it was over. The Israeli needed a man, not a boy. A husband and father for her children if she was ever to free herself from "Everybody's Best Friend," the controlling Abe.

Kalich spent the next six months in bed crying, with only his twin at his bedside to hold his hand, wipe away his tears, and tell him the fraternal "I told you so's" The following two and half years, he walked the city streets like a zombie. Ironically, maybe not so ironically, "Everybody's Best Friend," the charismatic Abe, became Kalich's and his brother's best friend.

Hana, age seventeen, Israel

Hana in New York City

Kalich's second great love came thirty-three years later with a 20-year-old Bulgarian who had won a music scholarship to Juilliard School. Exhibiting a ferocious will and calculated determination, augmented by shouts, screams and threats of suicide, she had swayed her parents to give her five hundred dollars so that she could come to New York and study the harp. First, though, she had to promise on all that was holy that she would be successful and, after attaining her American Dream, reciprocate by supporting them and her deaf younger sister for the rest of their lives. The reason Kalich fell in love with the young woman was not because her bone structure and facial features reminded him of the Israeli, which they did, but because every day after classes, at exactly 1 p.m., she would appear at his door and after her initial, Hi, how are you, sticking her hand out like a gun, she would seat herself in his rocking chair, surreptitiously cover her bosom and legs with her beige raincoat, and listen for four hours to Kalich talk about his favorite subject: himself.

Kalich took pains to speak slowly and simply, The Harpist was not yet fluent in English. It was the first time he had spoken to anyone, much less a beautiful young woman, in such an intimate manner since the Israeli. That along with holding her hand (another intimacy he had not experienced since the Israeli) and taking occasional strolls in Central Park (he had never done that either, even though he resided across the street from the greenery) proved fatal. The fifty-seven-year-old Kalich was no match for the young woman. His heart soon followed his words. The young woman could hardly reciprocate. All she could offer in return were brush kisses and aborted hugs, and after a certain quota, at a certain time, she would race off to her harp jobs (admittedly, she possessed a nearly pathologically obsessed work ethic); late night homework; student parties; sundry boyfriends: first Jason, then Alex, then Will. No doubt, Kalich never knew one complete and happy day. Not once in all the years with her did he find contentment, peace of mind, completion. The Young Harpist was always with him, but never his.

And on those occasions when Pia did offer herself to him, lying passively, obeisantly, on his bed trundle, it was Kalich who could not consummate. His body was tired. All those accumulated disappointments and failures in his life had taken their toll. All he could do was lay his hand on her face and bosom and stroke her gently, ever so gently. Those strokes meant everything to him. Were both an affirmation and a negation. A double-edged sword. In equal dosages, he experienced the highest heights and the bottomless despair of an aging man's love. It was as if all he had missed out on in his life, his avoidance of intimacy, living half-a-life, was now concentrated in these sad, pathetic, impotent gestures. The gently loving strokes both humiliated him, while at the same time allowed him to reach highs he had not even known with the Israeli thirty-three years before.

On those rare occasions when he couldn't hold his frustration in any longer, he would exclaim as much to himself as to The Harpist: No man ever gave more and got less.

But all his self-pitying outbursts would evoke was: Dick, you're a hundred years old!

Or: You waited too long.

Or: I want to be married for fifty years like my parents and have kids to love.

And then after a minute or two with a little girl's pout: Why couldn't my father be like you?

It goes without saying that Kalich was as oblivious to her retorts as The Harpist was to his plaints.

Perhaps his twin said it best:

You're an idiot. Any normal, healthy person would have left after the first date when she left you after dinner to meet her twenty-two-year-old boyfriend.

And that wasn't the worst of it. The worst was Kalich knew that the second greatest love of his life, a love he had waited thirty-three years for, was all in his mind.

Finally, after seven years of misery and humiliation, the sixty-four-year-old Kalich found the strength to accept The Young Harpist as a friend.

*The Young Harpist
on Robert Kalich's
terrace, 1994*

*Juilliard Concert,
1996*

Almost immediately, in the next four years, Kalich wrote two novels.

Charlie P—a novel about a man who lives his life by not living it.

And

Penthouse F—originally titled *Transfiguration of the Commonplace*—the novel he first envisioned twenty-five years earlier, the day he finished *The Nihilesthete*.

Both novels received generous attention from the literati.

The following morning Kalich read the previous day's pages. They're a little self-conscious, he thinks. Even re-mindful of his first novel, *My Father the Cantor*, which he wrote when twenty-six and which his twin summarized as though intelligent, the worst piece of constipated, self-conscious garbage he'd ever read. As an addendum, he added: It only goes to show how fucked up you are. It's more about you as a person than as a writer, and with these pages the two have met. Kalich agreed with him then and does so now. These pages are of a different tone than what he's striving for with this novel. Still, they do speak honestly about who he was at the time. And what he went through in his Molière tragi-comedies with both Hana and Pia. More importantly, the pages are a good example of what he is trying to come to grips with in his present effort: the Mind-Body Split. For that reason, he decides to let the pages stay. If nothing else, they will serve as a constant reminder of how easy it is for him to revert to type.

Kalich has always believed that what he knows, nobody knows. What everybody knows, he does not.

Kalich was wrong to marry the Israeli and The Young Harpist together. True, they comprise the two great loves of his life, but he has done both a disservice by suggesting that their contributions to his present novel were of equal import. To say that they serve as a warning of how easy it would be for him to revert to type is nothing but an insult to each and a trivialization altogether.

The Israeli, as we know, taught him about The Body: a young man's love. About passion and sex; joy and laughter; sorrow and tears. But it was The Young Harpist who taught him about The Mind. About the games it plays; its tricks and betrayals; and most of all, about its delusory readiness to make of experience what it will. By withholding her favors she taught the aging Kalich about hunger and want, yearning and loving—and he wanted and loved Pia at least as much as he wanted and loved Hana—about all he had missed out on in life and what, now, he could never have.

To be sure, it was The Young Harpist and not the Israeli, nor for that matter any special gift or metaphoric image (as some literary pundits would have you believe), who informed or rather deformed his heart and allowed him to see and now possibly create his present novel: *Mother Love*.

Oddly enough, only after conjuring these scribblings does Kalich feel better. So much so, he can hardly wait to share his findings with his character, the malevolent Haberman, and see how he will translate them from Kalich's mind to the page.

The words won't come. Kalich knows what he wants to say, but he cannot say it.

This is something very different than what Kalich has experienced most of his life. His terror of art, as he fancifully called it. What others know as writer's block. This problem is deeper. Doesn't originate from the outside. Has little to do with his lifelong fear of failure and judgment. It's nothing that simple. He is well past what the world thinks of him. This terror emanates from a deeper root.

This is not a novel about the Terror of Art.

This is a novel about the Terror of Life.

The truth is the world has already passed judgment on Kalich. Other than a motley crew of intellectuals and literati, the world places little value on who he is and what he has wrought. His name will not hang high in the literary rafters. His tomb will not be buried on hallowed ground. His books will not be found on shelves with other literary immortals. No. The problem has to do with The Self. It has ontic roots and causes. And with the loss of his powers, his value and worth, not only as a writer but as a person, are in jeopardy. His core identity is at stake. His very sense of self is in peril. For the first time in all his years, Kalich is a non-person.

Kalich does not know what to do about it. If he cannot write, it is the same—as the Austrian says—as not being able to breathe.

Still, this book is different than those which have come before it. Not the product of a single metaphoric image. With this effort it's more like coming together piecemeal. Paragraph by paragraph. Page by page. It's the way his twin describes his own writing process: constant surprise. Never knowing where he's going or even what his next sentence will be. Kalich is no different than so many other writers, starting with a word, a character, a sentence—he does not have the benefit of seeing the novel whole.

For a time, he does nothing except take shallow breaths. After three days, his lungs clear. He returns to his IBM Selectric. He can breathe again.

Kalich chooses Peter Handke's *The Afternoon of a Writer* as one of his one hundred favorite books.

It will sit as number eleven on the shelf.

Kalich intends to spend the whole day trashing books.

One cannot spend the whole day trashing books.

Kalich trashed his Swiss-German-Austrian collection this afternoon. At least twelve hundred books accumulated over a lifetime. From Goethe and Schiller, through Mann, Hesse, Musil, Broch, Rilke, Canetti, Boll, Grass, Frisch, Bernhard, and Handke.

As previously stated—Franz Kafka has his own shelf.

Quite a collection, Kalich thinks. All that genius and artistry, and yet... even one of their greatest minds, Martin Heidegger, turned fasc...

(Kalich does not finish the sentence.)

Before any other, Kalich chooses Herman Hesse's *Steppenwolf* for his favorite bookshelf. Hesse's novel made the strongest impression on Kalich when he was in his late twenties. At that time, he didn't know where he stood. Was he a writer or a dilettante? An artist or an aesthete? Like Harry Haller, Hesse's character in *Steppenwolf*, Kalich was a man outside. On the periphery. Even today, no matter how much his actual life has changed, and he's personally grown, this affliction remains. Each and every time he sits at his IBM Selectric and is ready to write, it's always...

... as if for the first time.

In addition to *Steppenwolf*, Kalich chooses two authors

of opposite poles: Max Frisch and Thomas Bernhard. In all his years of reading, he has never known a writer who removed himself so completely, so utterly, from his narratives as Frisch. Wholly impersonal, rigorously devoid of any confessionalism as one critic put it: the objective; and Bernhard, wholly subjective and impassioned. Kalich selected Frisch's diary *Sketchbook, 1966-1971* and Thomas Bernhard's *Concrete*, a novel about a man suffering from writer's block.

Kalich had the good fortune to meet Max Frisch in New York the same year he finished *The Nihilesthete*. He was introduced by Michael Roloff, a well-regarded German intellectual who had translated such estimable novelists as Herman Hesse and Peter Handke, and whose opinion carried weight. Frisch agreed to read Kalich's novel. A week later, Kalich received his call: Herr Kalich, Herr Kalich, I want you to take what I say seriously, and not seriously at all. I've now read your novel *Nihilesthete*. It's powerful, yes. Very powerful for an American, but the metaphor is a little crude, don't you think?

Taken aback by Frisch's words—they struck Kalich as a verbal cul-de-sac; a catatonic's double bind—he could only offer the feeble response: Max, compared to your own fictions, all metaphoric fiction today, including my own, must seem crude.

But the words stuck with Kalich. The more he thought about them, the more he came to believe that Frisch had purposefully made use of such parabolic literary tenets as paradox, illogic, and apparent contradiction to free Kalich from linear thinking—to open Kalich to possibilities beyond the yoke of reason.

It should be noted that twenty-nine years later, Kalich paraphrased Frisch's words, word for word, in his novel *Penthouse F.*

And today, seven years after *Penthouse F* was published and eight years since he first saw Mother and the boy on the street, Kalich finally feels sufficiently confident to put theory to practice and give his utmost to creating his ongoing book, *The Assisted Living Facility Library.*

Taking the boy by the hand, early this morning, Haberman heads out the door. The walk will serve more than several purposes: on the one hand, it will afford Haberman much-needed exercise, and with his advancing years, he needs it. Two, it can only further help bond him with the boy. But even more importantly, it will make Mother more concerned and anxious. What is the old man doing, saying to the boy? Mother will feel even more isolated and alone. Her tiny space will become even smaller.

Haberman is very much aware that this tiny space is fast becoming Mother's whole world.

There is another benefit. When they return from the walk and the boy can't wait to talk, and speaks in excited, yet whispered tones about all they experienced together, all he has shared with Haberman, and Mother is not privy to—Haberman is not sufficiently gifted with words, as Kalich is, to adequately describe how it is not the boy's happiness and glee, but Mother's mind and body frozen at half-mast that gives him the greatest pleasure.

The more hours the book dealer spends on the street, the less he seems to sell.

Kalich was saddened for Charlie.

Despite the fact that there were numerous passersby on the street, not one gave as much as the slightest glance at Charlie or his books. One did flip through a *Playboy* magazine, circa 1960, and another the pages of a *Life* magazine, showing Eisenhower on the cover. And a third even purchased two of the vintage framed advertisement photos which Charlie, of late, much to his distemper, had begun laying on the ground in front of the bookcases. The photos purchased were: Billy Rose's Aquacade, New York World's Fair, 1939 (admission fifteen cents), highlighted by a bathing suit model; and a Jackie Boy Brand, displaying a smiling sailor boy holding an orange. Copyright, 1923.

Charlie was happy to make the sale.

Admittedly, writers have a cruel streak, and Kalich is no exception.

How's the book business?

You call this a business? Charlie answers, biting fiercely on his long, obese cigar.

Kalich can't help himself:

Then why do it? It's not like you're a writer and have no choice.

A cigar-chomping silence follows...

...Kalich needs no more. He has his next chapter.

Much to Kalich's surprise, and he would think his readers, too, he has kept up a meaningful relationship, perhaps the only such friendship left in his life, with the Harpist for the past twenty-three years. They meet regularly for lunches and dinners, and she never fails to invite him to her Greenwich home on Christmas to visit her and her husband, a successful investor, and two girls, Yvette, 7, Thea, 9, and on other occasions as well. Recently, for the sake of his novel, he asked her if being a mother was all she expected it to be when she was twenty.

Don't hold back, he said. Don't worry about grammar or syntax. Just let your heart pour out what you really feel.

The following morning, Kalich received this email:

- - - - - - Original Message - - - - - -
Subject: Re: Mother Love
From: Pia@Yahoo.com
Date: Sat, September 23, 2017 8:39 AM
To: Kalich@gmail.com

I go in the morning to wake them up and start kissing them,
overwhelmed by their beauty and unawareness...
Almost as a robber taking advantage and "drinking" on beauty
when no one is watching...
I kiss every inch of their faces, arms, shoulders whatever is
sticking on top of blankets.. they slowly start waking up and
moving, trying to get away from me and also offering me new
places to kiss...
Back, neck... Their unaware, sleepy stage appeals to my primal
animal instincts... Their soft skin
I want to lay down and hold them and kiss them a ton more,
and never let this moment end...
almost forgetting i am just waking them up for school...
and then like a robber again, I quickly run away from that
"heavenly" experience...

Love,
Pia

Thea, age 7

Yvette, age 9

Something deep inside Kalich has been stirring recently. A push and pull, an inner tension...

What does it mean?

What could it be?

Is it time already to bring his character Haberman above ground? If for no other reason than to see just where and how Haberman will guide him. Make certain he will not go astray in his exploration of Mother and the boy.

When Kalich first envisioned this book, for lack of courage or whatever one might call it, he let it foment inside him for eight long years. And now, having started the book in earnest five weeks ago, he has 100 pages, but still, there are times when he has no idea what to write. Where to go. What comes next. Kalich would be the first to admit he needs all the help he can get. And, of course, he has always felt that his character, Haberman, would make an ideal partner. As worthy a candidate as any he has ever known, or even read about.

In fear and trembling, in his mind if not body, in his imagination if not book, Kalich lets Haberman out of his cage. Kalich and Haberman will work through their most dreaded fears, most difficult and darkest hours together.

Is this not what Kalich has struggled with all along? To make what is dark light? What is unknowable knowable? To merge and marry mind and body; the inner and outer; to become one with his characters, and together as equal partners with equal say, create their narrative together?

Kalich and Haberman, author and character, will spend next Sunday in the park playing their games on Mother and the boy.

Kalich is fully aware that this is not the same as taking dictation as he did with his novel *The Nihilesthete.* For that novel all he had to do was be awakened by his muse in the wee hours and transcribe those dreamlike images to the light of day.

But this time, for this work, Kalich is grappling with the questions: are art and life, fiction and reality, author and character—the same? Different? One and the same?

On a more personal level Kalich is questioning: why can't he translate his body consciousness to real life? Why has his alter-ego, the demonic Haberman, remained only in his mind? Why has that dimension of himself been confined only to his fiction writing? And most importantly, as he has said from the start—why can't he, Kalich, be more, live more, than the life of the mind, the half-a-life (as his brother deems it) he has known up to now?

For the first time in all his years of writing, Kalich thinks this collaborative experience might prove to be fun. Like his twin brother has countless times said: Writing should be fun, enjoyable, liberating.

Kalich knows his twin would be happy for him.

Not only Mother and the boy, but Kalich and Haberman, like a family, are counting the days until Sunday, and not figuratively but literally.

Having entered the park by the 59th Street and Fifth Avenue entrance, Kalich was about to direct Mother to a park bench between the lake and sloping grass hill where the greatest concentration of activity takes place on Sunday when, almost immediately, Haberman exerted his influence. No, he said, Mother must be able to see and hear the boy at all times. But not everything. Just enough to pique her interest. If, for example, the boy were to howl with laughter at a man carrying a monkey playing a small accordion on his back, she should be able to hear his laughter and the monkey's music, but not see the accordion or recognize the tune. And under no circumstance should she be allowed to leave her bench seat or be able to participate in the day's activities. It will be like pouring salt on the wound. Mother's frustrations and disappointments will be all the more punishing and cruel.

Kalich agrees. No doubt this is Haberman's calling. As difficult as it might be for him, Kalich resolves to give Haberman free rein.

But how could he have missed that? If nothing else, he should have learned that much from The Young Harpist.

More than ever, Kalich is confident that by choosing Haberman to partner with, he has chosen well.

Kalich catches himself. He is nearly as curious as Haberman. He has neglected to inform the reader of Mother's reaction to being told that she would not be permitted to leave her bench seat and, even more so, to participate in the day's activities.

Needless to say, once again, as always, her shoulders slumped, and facial muscles sagged.

Though on further reflection, Kalich believes this is a good thing. It only goes to show how close he and his partner have become.

Now where to begin? So much to choose from. There are enough games here to fill a thousand Sundays.

Haberman tosses a Frisbee to the boy. (Kalich has purchased enough bats and balls and everything else he deemed necessary to field an entire team.)

The partners play Frisbee with the boy who chases along like a dog after a stick. By the way mother jerks her head back and forth, to and fro, Kalich can tell she is following their every move. If she doesn't seem particularly glum, she's not happy either. Certainly, there is no smile on her face.

(Then again catatonics rarely smile.)

Soon enough, they make their way down the hill to a nearby bench. Kalich cannot help but notice the au pairs wheeling their baby carriages, chattering non-stop to their charges. Some not more than four to six months old. Certainly, the babies cannot speak back, much less understand, and, yet, the women go on chattering. What could they be speaking about? As he has thought all his life, the au pairs are not really speaking. Like the babies, they are just making sounds.

Kalich has disdained such chatter all his life?

Other au pairs join in. From Jamaica, Panama, Dominican Republic, as far off as Africa and Norway: all partaking in the same chatter. Kalich cannot comprehend what they are talking about. Whatever it is, they seem as much invested, more connected, than so many of his own past conversations held with peers, colleagues and friends.

And why are the women so happy?

From the way Mother is looking at the au pairs, Kalich guesses that she would like to join in the conversation.

But what has Mother to say?

Does it really matter?

Passing a woman reading a book on a bench, Kalich can't help himself and cranes his neck to discern the book's title. Disappointed: a book without hesitation he would consign to the trash pile.

But one thought leads to another. Kalich notices he does not have a book of his own in his hand. Is that progress? Is he so taken up with Mother and the boy that he has no need for a book?

Just posing the question gives him all the answer he needs.

Kalich recalls his old history professor at City College saying to his class, "How many of you when reading a book and coming across a word you don't understand, take the time to get up from your seat and go to a dictionary?" The professor's words sounded more like an injunction than mere advice or recommendation.

From that day on, Kalich has carried a pocket-sized Web-

ster's dictionary on his person.

With as severe an expression on his face as Kalich has ever seen (or written), Haberman takes the boy by the hand and leads him to the mountainous rock boulder where older, more agile and physically mature children climb and play. Encouraged by Haberman, the boy climbs his way to the top.

Mother, with prodigious effort, somehow manages to stand erect. Her usually expressionless face contorts in fear as she watches Haberman lift his arms, beckoning the boy to—

Haberman was right to allow Mother to both see and hear, but not participate. Not only has it made her Sunday in the park, as he said it would, all the more cruel and punishing, but just as importantly it has made the partners' all the more interesting and enjoyable.

Certainly, it has given Kalich something to write about.

Two young lovers pass by. Stop to embrace. Walk a few steps further, stop, kiss, and embrace again.

When was the last time Kalich was kissed by a young woman like that?

And when the boy stares and points his finger at the great white bird sitting on the tree branch across the lake, Mother can only wonder what is capturing his attention so.

And later, on the way home, when the boy races to the water's edge to see a beady-eyed frog peering out at the lake, and a wriggling fish raising its head out of the water for food, and the boy stares likewise beady-eyed, once again Mother has no inkling as to what provokes him so.

Haberman has calculated his sight angles well. From where Mother sits, no matter how high she stands or stretches her torso from her ball and chain seating arrangement—it is never enough. Though she is able to see and hear the boy at all times, she is not able to see and hear everything.

Oh, Mother, how can you place your most precious possession, the boy, in the hands of two strangers?

What if the boy drinks too much soda pop, eats too much ice cream and cotton candy, causing a tummy ache?

What if racing down the slope, playing Frisbee or chasing a ball, the boy falls, scrapes his knee, breaks his neck?

What if the park attendant, driving his truck to empty the garbage can, doesn't see the boy because of his diminutive size?

What if the boy, in his exuberant youth, follows the beautiful Asian bride in her wedding dress and the proud smiling groom in his tuxedo up the winding road and gets lost in the madding crowd?

Oh, Mother, when will you learn that you must be on constant vigil? In an instant sunshine can turn to rain and Sunday in the park can turn to tragedy and pain.

After Haberman has taken his leave, Kalich makes his way into Mother's space. She is standing bent over, facing the wall with her usual dead-eyed stare. Her supper remains untouched on a makeshift table. Nudging her gently by the elbow, Kalich leads her to a chair at the table. Smiling, he utters: So, Mother, did you enjoy our little family outing today? Mother peers at him. There is a rippling beneath the still water surface. If only for an instant, Kalich feels whole. What was previously reserved only for his fictions, now for the first time by dint of will and daring, he feels he and Haberman are one.

In Kalich's youth, it was his opinion that the American novel was fifty years behind the European. And even at this wizened age, he is not embarrassed to say, to an extent, he still feels the same. But still, with all his reading, he has come to realize that in every country's haystack a gem or two can be found. And, to be sure, the Americans have had their share. Writers such as Ernest Hemingway; Virginia Woolf; Saul Bellow; William Gaddis; James Baldwin; John Barth; and many many more have all lived up to that lofty status.

And so today, exerting painstaking effort, and after having spent the better part of the morning and early afternoon clearing out his American section, some six hundred books, he finds himself left with five books he feels sufficiently worthy to accompany him to the Assisted Living Facility.

They are: Nathaniel West's *Miss Lonelyhearts* and David Markson's final four books, which marked a turning point in the author's career:

Reader's Block

This is Not a Novel
Vanishing Point
and
The Last Novel

Miss Lonelyhearts: Kalich's favorite American novel—
spawned in the soil of the Great Depression. So much
of the novel reminded Kalich of his own novel, *The
Nihilesthete*. The newspaper writer assigned to write
the Agony Column to answer the letters of "Desper-
ate," "Sick-of-it-all," "Disillusioned"; the hateful editor,
Shrike, who destroys the reporter's idealistic offerings
of art-sex-religion to the suffering.

There was no doubt in Kalich's mind that West's apoca-
lyptic vision of the Great Depression went further,
mined deeper, than any of his contemporaries, including Fitzgerald and Steinbeck, in satirizing his era's dark,
bleak American soil.

But was West's vision really so different from Kalich's
nihilistic vision of his own era's spiritually diminished
time? The confrontation between the inwardly dead-
ened caseworker, Haberman, whose mission was to
destroy Brodski—a limbless, mentally diagnosed idiot
who cannot speak, except in cat's meows, yet metaphorically symbolizes the last bastion of spiritual fe-

cundity—an artist whose transcendent quest serves as a revelatory mirror to all the caseworker is not.

Kalich even felt West's actual life paralleled his own. Entering Brown University, a privileged youth, leaving it four years later penniless. His father, a real estate mogul, lost everything in the Depression, and though West's four novels (two of them American classics: *Miss Lonelyhearts* and *The Day of the Locust*) gained critical acclaim, they never even remotely found a readership; certainly nothing compared to Hemingway or Steinbeck. Like Kalich, but for different reasons, West resorted to writing musical acts and film treatments, only to be met with Hollywood rejection letters and failure. Finally, after years, he found love, was making progress in Hollywood, and was even committed to writing a big novel, more expansive and ambitious than anything he had created before, when he died in a car crash at thirty-seven.

Whether Kalich's novel *The Nihilesthete* is comparable to *Miss Lonelyhearts,* we don't know (one can never be certain about such things, least of all the author), but we do know Kalich has said many times he could only hope that, with the passing years, one day *The Nihilesthete* would sit on the same shelf as, or perhaps more realistically on a neighboring shelf to, *Miss Lonelyhearts*.

When Kalich finished his novel *Charlie P*, the first person he contacted to read the novel was David Markson at his Greenwich Village apartment. Though Kalich didn't know Markson personally, he was well-acquainted with his novels and felt if anyone would be sympathetic to his work, it would be him. Markson didn't pull punches and immediately told Kalich he could not read the novel. He was sick with cancer, half blind, and working on his own novel.

Appreciating his directness, Kalich prolonged the conversation, the pair hit it off, and as the months passed, Kalich grew to like the man, almost as much as his books.

What impressed Kalich was the welcoming warmth of the writer. In their very first conversation, Markson asked Kalich how old he was. Kalich, who was in his early sixties at the time and never told anyone his age, answered Markson. Markson's instant reply was: You're a baby.

He repeated the phrase numerous times in the ensuing years. The older writer's words were spoken with such playfulness and understanding that a kindred connection was born from the start.

Another quality that struck Kalich was that even though Markson had already written an acknowledged masterpiece, *Wittgenstein's Mistress*, years earlier, he was as self-doubting and questioning about his work as Kalich was. Markson would regularly ask Kalich: Do you think I should write another novel like my last three? Kalich would always answer the same: Yes, I do. Other than *Wittgenstein's Mistress,* it's what you're known for.

Markson would turn silent, mute, taking the words in like stones falling in a river.

And, of course, there was also the fact that Markson was destitute at the time. (That was easy for Kalich to identify with.) The aging writer would hardly ever take the subway or bus but would walk the city streets to most anywhere his destination was. Eventually, Kalich offered him money to ease the burden, but he would not accept. If it came to that, he had other people to go to.

Another quality Kalich appreciated about Markson was all the time he spent researching his next novel (aptly titled *The Last Novel*)...

—which would, like his previous three novels, prove

unprecedented, virtually obliterate the conventions of the modern novel: Like other literary explorers, he made the form of the novel to a good extent its subject.

He was widely generous, perhaps compulsively so, about sharing his thought process.

After Kalich's twin, at his strong urging, read Markson's last three novels, he immediately called him. They're gimmicks. You can't compare him to a Bellow or any legitimate novelist, he scoffed. Of course, you like him. He's as weird as you. And like you, he will sell a hundred books if he's lucky.

And, of course, Kalich's twin was right. You couldn't compare Markson to a traditional novelist. But he was wrong, too. Markson was writing a novel by not writing it. Plotless, characterless, action-less: even without a subject.

Kalich's thought at the time was—he should be so fortunate to be as original as Markson.

A recurring dialectic between Markson and Kalich was how bored each of them was by conventional storytelling. Artifice, Markson called it. Kalich termed it melodrama.

At some point, Kalich would good-naturedly tease the elderly novelist by calling his attention to the fact that in one of his three novels, and now with this work-in-progress, he was still making use of the word "novel." Of course, I am, Markson would adamantly respond. Why not? That's what they are: novels.

Old, half-blind, fighting cancer, the old writer could never let go of the titular and syntactic referential idea of the novel.

David Markson was the quintessential problematic man. He explored comically and in profound seriousness the ongoing and endless questions, torments, and struggles of self-conscious man.

In all fairness, it must be said that Kalich's twin did admire West's novella *Miss Lonelyhearts*, even if not as much as his more traditional-length novel, *The Day of the Locust*.

But as to the rest of Kalich's selections, he would have composed a very different list. If Kalich is cerebral, circumspect, economic, his twin is large, visceral, expansive; size matters most in everything he does.

How many nights did the two stay up arguing over the varying merits of Tolstoy and Chekhov. While Kalich loved Chekhov, to his twin the playwright was small, couldn't begin to compare to Tolstoy's majestic *War and Peace* and *Anna Karenina.* And the same for James Joyce's *Ulysses,* as against Kafka's mini-novel *The Metamorphosis.*

Another exception to the rule—Kalich's twin greatly valued Bernhard Malamud's *The Assistant*—he felt it had heart.

A quality he chronically berated Kalich for not having.

Kalich, in turn, considered his twin a sentimentalist.

But of all American novelists, and not unexpectedly, Kalich's twin loved the street fighter Norman Mailer the best. He had read Mailer's *The White Negro* his first year in college, and the essay had left an indelible mark. As we already know, the twins were differently made, opposite sides of the same coin. And their differences manifested themselves in almost every which way. For example, Kalich had amassed over a lifetime close to eight thousand books and had read many two, three, even five times, making lists of words and phrases culled from those books which for one reason or another caught his eye or he thought would make good titles for possible future books; his twin, by way of contrast, was as much a Book Collector as Book Lover. His library was at least double the size of Kalich's; perhaps containing more than fifteen thousand volumes and all unmarked, spotless, with many first editions. In fact, his twin had employed a retired bookstore owner in Colorado whose sole task was to find those rare books neither he nor anybody else could.

But for Kalich, Mailer with all his vitality and pugilist's energy, and despite possessing one of the most fertile literary minds of his generation, still lacked what he considered the most essential quality for a novelist: a philosophic center. A tight-lipped particularity which allowed its bearer to make the leap to the universal. For that reason, he could not compete with the truly great, Kalich's two favorites: Albert Camus and Pär Lagerkvist.

The French Nobel laureate Albert Camus' *The Fall* saw through the first half of the twentieth century's rationalizing self-deceptions. Perhaps even more significant to the writer, Kalich, it showed how a story could be told. Camus makes "you," the reader, into a character in his confessional narrative and by the end of the book his character, Jean Baptiste, becomes not only "you" but the universal everybody. No less impressive is the Swedish Nobel laureate, Pär Lagerkvist, who captured the nature of evil by dint of a single metaphoric image in his novel (and character) *The Dwarf.*

It should be noted both books stand side by side, ranking one and two, on Kalich's favorite bookshelf and most definitely will accompany him to the Assisted Living Facility.

Kalich's Favorite Bookshelf

Kalich thought it a good idea, and has taken the time, to create a chart (for which we are thankful) that shows with very little doubt the contrasting book preferences between him and his twin brother:

ROBERT KALICH

Moby Dick
  by Herman Melville
Ulysses
  by James Joyce
The Grapes of Wrath
  by John Steinbeck
The Magic Mountain
  by Thomas Mann
Herzog by Saul Bellow
The Brothers Karamazov
  by Fyodor Dostoevsky
Love in the Time of Cholera
  by Gabriel García Márquez
Beloved by Toni Morrison
Life: A User's Manual
  by Georges Perec
The Trial by Franz Kafka
Anna Karenina
  by Leo Tolstoy

RICHARD KALICH

Old Man and the Sea
  by Ernest Hemingway
*Portrait of the Artist as a Young
  Man* by James Joyce
Of Mice and Men
  by John Steinbeck
Death in Venice
  by Thomas Mann
Seize the Day by Saul Bellow
Notes from the Underground
  by Fyodor Dostoevsky
Book of Imaginary Beings
  by Jorge Luis Borges
A Mercy by Toni Morrison
Virtually any short story
  written by Alice Munro
Metamorphosis by Franz Kafka
The Death of Ivan Ilyich
  by Leo Tolstoy

Kalich and Haberman spend a good deal of time together. It's not that they enjoy each other's company so much as they recognize their union complexes and enriches the games they conceive, plan, and play together...

...always at Mother's expense.

Mother will never be allowed to feed the boy. Nor will she be allowed to sleep with him. Gaze at him while he sleeps. Talk to him unless under the full supervision of one or both of the partners.

Though the partners might have missed out on the boy's first steps, first words, both agree there's more than ample time to make up for it now.

Time passes so quickly during these playdates that one feels safe to say that the partners are investing themselves completely.

Kalich is captivated by the way the boy's face knits in concentration and serious deliberation while selecting a toy to play with from the large corrugated box filled to bursting with games, toys, and modular figures. Then, after choosing, turning to Kalich, Haberman, or both, he says: Let's play. Haberman prizes the look, somewhere between perplexity and tears, that comes over the boy's face when he triumphs over the boy in a game.

Most certainly, Mother feels not only left out, but hurt in both cases.

Kalich has to constantly remind him to eat slowly; to chew each bite deliberately. With Haberman, it's the opposite. The boy refuses to swallow the food and his right cheek swells into a large ball pouch. Either way, both men seem more than satisfied as long as Mother cannot partake.

(One would be remiss not to mention that the boy loves desserts. Chocolate ice cream having taken over chocolate pudding as his favorite.)

Gazing at the boy while asleep brings equal pleasure to the partners. After all, who could be so callous as not to be enthralled by a sleeping child? Still, one cannot help but think that Mother craning her neck to peek in now and again only adds to their pleasure.

Why else would the curtain drapes be partially loosened, and the door left partially opened?

Kalich holds the boy's little thumb when sleeping (as he did with the Israeli's son). Haberman, for his own reasons, doesn't touch the boy at all.

Even though the boy can hardly count, he is not too young to squeal with delight and clap his hands every time Haberman, Kalich, or both deposit a coin or two into his piggy bank. He could never receive such generosity from Mother. She doesn't have the means. "He's a born businessman," says Kalich. "He won't end up on the street like his mother," retorts Haberman, just loud enough for Mother to hear.

If the boy awakes in the middle of the night from a nightmare or just has the need to cuddle, it is Kalich's bed (which on occasion he shares with Haberman) he races to. Of course, we already know Mother's curtain window remains just open enough for her to view the hugs and kisses shared by Kalich, if not Haberman, with the boy.

On his birthday—the day is his. Anything he wants to do. Whether in the park, sandbox, at the movies, blowing out candles, or receiving presents at his birthday party— it is only Kalich and Haberman who bestow such bounty. Mother is nowhere to be found.

And it is the same at Christmas. Santa may come through the chimney to fill the boy's stockings hanging over the fireplace with gifts and presents, but, again, it is only the boy who will be there to greet Santa—that is, the partners dressed in Santa's garb. Mother is nowhere to be found.

To his credit, it should be said that Kalich truly enjoys tickling the child's tummy and hearing his giggling response. But more than once Haberman has had to remind him that it is all to no avail unless Mother is made privy to the child's delight. And one can be certain she is.

When Kalich was small and jumped into the pool at the Catskill Mountains hotel where his parents spent their annual four-week summer vacation, he would always first run by his mother and shout, "Mommy, watch me!" And so, it is the same now with the boy. The only difference is it is not to Mother, but to Kalich and Haberman he shouts, "Watch me!"

When the boy has a tummy ache, there is nothing Haberman finds more amusing than watching Kalich, per his instruction, as a doctor to a nurse, lift the boy's legs up to his chest to let out gas. "Feel better," he says. When the boy's eyes open wide, first in surprise, then astonishment, the partners, like the boy, must feel they are possessed with demonic powers.

Mother, on the other hand, has a different interpretation. By the horrific look on her face, either by some ancient maternal instinct or collective memory, it doesn't seem too farfetched to conclude that the partners' demonic powers could include having the boy tossed to his death from a mountain cliff as sacrificial ritual to the Gods.

Let it not be lost that Mother receives priority seating for this event's proceedings.

No longer does Kalich not know where to take the narrative. He is nearly halfway home and for the first time he sees the book's shape and arc. At times, he can even sense a shadowy glimmer of the end. It is not so much a matter of getting there any longer—the question now is whether he has the courage to persevere with his original vision. Not whether he can write the fiction, but whether he can live it.

To that end, we already know that Kalich has partnered with his character, Haberman. And that the demands of this work are far more challenging than in *The Nihilesthete*. Kalich knows to realize the transformation in full, he would not only have to merge and marry character and author, Haberman and Kalich, as an imagined fiction in his mind, but to literally become Haberman in real life.

From the start, Kalich understood that this challenge would test his limits, both as a writer and as a man.

But can such a transformation even take place? And if so, how will it happen? At this point, Kalich is still in muddy waters. The ensuing images and the ending are obscure. For certain, he still has not been able to transpose the climax (or anticlimax) of his vision to conscious thought.

Much less the written page.

True, he has a glimmer, an evanescent shading on the periphery of consciousness, guiding him with intuition and shadowy intimations. But little more than that. His explorations of the book's landscape hardly go further. But now, as compared to when he started, although he still does not have a clear path, certainly his mind and some of his plot machinations are no longer shrouded in mist.

Kalich knows where he is going, even if he still is not certain how to get there.

From this juncture on, all that Kalich has lost due to age and, more recently in the last several decades, with the usurpation of the literary culture by the digital culture, the word by the image, all that gave his life value and meaning—in short, his frustration with who he has become will for the most part now be shown by Kalich and Haberman concentrating their focus and venting their rages on Mother and the boy.

Kalich has not been sleeping or eating well of late. He's anxious about his work. It's not going well. He's all too aware that his body is not what it used to be. The demonic rages and inner violence that poured out of him when writing *The Nihilesthete* have been calmed with the passing years.

He has grave doubts whether he can make up for all he's lost and match the ending of *The Nihilesthete* with mere cunning and craft.

And at the same time (which only adds to his anxiety), he knows the book cannot stay—as one literary colleague has told him—"all in his mind."

Kalich called his twin this morning for solace.

You're unbelievable, he says. You just got to keep busy. Like with this bullshit book you've been talking about for eight years. You won't make a dollar on it. Why can't you just enjoy your life?!

After Kalich responded as best as he could, his brother retaliated: I got a great life: Knute. Brunde. Treat friends to dinner all the time. Gardening on my Central Park South terrace. Ballet. Movies. Concerts. Theater.

The Philharmonic. No financial pressure. Good health. I'm grateful. His voice quieted. He spoke nearly in a whisper. All those things don't mean anything to you. Never did.

It was difficult to tell if he was sad for Kalich or himself.

For the longest time, Kalich has promised Mother she could have an entire day to spend with the boy without having to share him with either Haberman or himself. Mother has looked forward to this day for so long, been promised it in so many different ways, that Kalich is beginning to fear that in Mother's addled mind the day has already come and gone.

Of course, as much as Mother has looked forward to this day, the partners have looked forward to it even more.

Please don't get the idea that Kalich wants to take all the credit for this very special day. He repeatedly has said that without Haberman at his side, making his singular contributions, the day could never even have been close to what he hoped it to be.

Fortunately, it turned out to be an especially beautiful day outside, but inside Mother's space it is sweltering with heat. The air conditioner has been turned off, the fuse in fact removed. One of the many conditions for Mother's privacy with her son is that she abide by the rules. Rules set in stone. Mother fully understands that she is not allowed to touch the air conditioner, neither turn it on nor off. Nor is she permitted to fan herself or the boy with her hands, much less avail herself of any prop or ploy.

Meanwhile, the partners are seated comfortably in their air-conditioned room, a surveillance camera recording on screen all of Mother's efforts to deal with her and the boy's ordeal.

With sweat dripping from every pore in their bodies, Mother proves a dexterous and formidable foe. She's not going to surrender without a fight. As usual, her maternal instincts and adaptive powers, evolved over eons of time, are truly impressive. Certainly, her antics hold the partners' attention.

This Mother, in particular, seems well-suited for the task.

Cupping her hands to catch the water falling from her body and the boy's, she makes every effort to bathe the boy in sweat. Spitting into her hands, she mixes saliva with a few shed tears and smears the boy with her own bath oil impasto. Laying him prostrate on the cool wooden floor proves just as futile, as the floor planks, now steaming with heat, feel more like burning hot coals. And there is no sink water. (There is no sink in Mother's space.) Not even toilet water. Coincidence or not, the toilet has been unusable for nearly as long as Kalich began promising Mother her special day and holds nothing but feces and urine. Perhaps, most painful of all, is Mother having to watch the boy cry dry tears and shout he wants to go back to Kalich and Haberman.

Still, Mother does not raise the white flag. Instead she scours the space for a dark place: a closet, windowsill, one of the four corners. Anything. While the heat remains unrelenting. Like a boxer who has endured twelve brutal rounds, body stooped, shoulders sagging, hands dropped to the knees, mouth dry, no more saliva to be spat out, her well gone dry, it finally dawns upon Mother's ancient maternal brain that despite all her efforts, there is no relief to be found.

And even if Mother has been promised a day with the boy—for how long can he continue to endure this suffocating heat?

For how long can she allow him to suffer?

Finally, and only after passing the boy an indecipherable glance, a what-am-I-to-do Sisyphean shrug-of-the-shoul-

ders, followed instantly by his nodding assent, Mother peeks her head through the curtain door and return the boy to the partners.

Once returned, the fuse is plugged back in, the air conditioner turned on, and without delay Mother (alone) and the boy (with the partners) can once again find relief from the cool air wafting through the apartment.

In the wee hours, Kalich and Haberman congratulate themselves for having turned Mother's special day not only into their sweetest victory, but Mother's greatest defeat.

Kalich's living room is unrecognizable. The books are torn from their moorings and, from the top shelf—Beckett; Joyce; Márquez; Perec—all through an entire side wall of seven tiers, eight columns, seating such favorites in the first column as: Coetze; Lagerkvist; West; Kundera; Gombrowicz; Pessoa; extending through French; German; Italian; Israeli; Polish; Holocaust fiction, and ending up in the eighth column with the Albanian, Ismael Kadare, and the Japanese, Kōbō Abe, are no longer to be found in their rightful place.

Nothing is where it should be.

No book is where it once was.

A mountainous pile of books takes up the entire center of the room. Once select books, highlighted by prime shelf space, now lie scattered like so much refuse and debris. In Kalich's kitchen, the literary criticism, biography, and scholarly works, such as Sven Birkerts's *An Artificial Wilderness* and Cynthia Ozick's books of essays, are missing altogether. And on the opposite wall, Kalich's earliest readings: the great psychologists Freud,

Adler, Jung, as well as his first forays into existential literature, beginning with the book *Existence* edited by Rollo May, have vanished as well. Kalich credits that book for not only leading him to existential psychology and philosophy, but to opening the trail to European writers en masse. Kalich felt an immediate and kindred affinity to the European novel. Perhaps it was the Europeans' voice, sensibility, their long history, pioneering the modern era in the seventeenth century, the death of God, the birth of the individual, art as the yardstick of personal worth and imagination, having fought wars and spilled blood on their own shores, and today, our present age, with their powers waning, their darker and deeper understanding of human existence than their American counterparts. Regardless, from that point on American fiction lost its special status for Kalich. Now as Kalich surveys his back room, he sees nothing but empty and upended bookshelves.

Nothing is more empty than a bookshelf without books, he thinks.

The closet nearest to the kitchen, used as an office supply room and, most importantly, harboring his Book of Quotes; Rejection Letters; Publishing Contracts; Book Reviews miserly collected over a lifetime (or at least since *The Nihilesthete* was first published), is now in disarray. A United States postal service priority envelope, actually two, usually filled to bursting with all the pay stubs he received from his many years working as a Caseworker for the Department of Social Services, has also torn apart and the pay stubs, like all else, lie scattered about. Kalich knows better than anyone what those soul-deadening civil service years cost him: time clocks; procedures; supervisors; bureaucratic meetings; and more importantly he knows he has no one to blame for those years but himself. Upon retirement, his goal was to paper his bathroom walls with the check stubs. But fifteen years later he still has not gotten around to it.

Almost accidentally, he finds lying in a hollowed recess a manila envelope containing typewritten pages, numbered, dated and listing novels; screenplays; treatments—each and every submission giving him so much hope and possibility at that time in his life. There are also landmark letters from literary luminaries, such as Joseph Brodsky; Sven Birkerts; Max Frisch; Susan Sontag; Warren Motte; Brian McHale; as well as from publishers and scholars, that have additionally been ruined by time and wear. So much paper gone berserk. Intermingling with office supplies and sprawled pages: possibly from his Book of Quotes or a once favored title. Here and there a rejection letter is found (three months waiting and hope); a book review (which justified his life). Nothing is ordered. Nothing is logically placed. All is a potpourri of chance and whim, random and careless tossing of books and paper. There is no rhyme or reason to any of it. After a lifetime questing after purpose and meaning, nothing is left but a miasma of disarray and chaos.

That night the building manager visited Kalich. A hardworking man who left a destitute life in Ireland with a young wife to forge a new start in New York. Today, twenty-five years later, he and his wife have three sons—all superintendents of elite buildings in Mid-Manhattan. Having survived nightmarish bouts of alcoholism, he now heads a recovery program for alcoholics and additionally relocates those who show promise with jobs as concierges, doormen, handymen, and other such work in his and colleagues' buildings. When Kalich asked him what would happen to his books once he's gone, the building manager retorted, Not much. Not in the condition you left them.

Then, taking a deep sigh, he added: But you of all people know nobody reads any longer. And those that do, certainly don't read the books you've read.

Kalich selects Tarjei Vesaas' *The Ice Palace,* Witold

Gombrowicz's *Pornografia,* and Kōbō Abe's *The Face of Another* for the Assisted Living Facility Library.

Kalich needs to take a day for himself. He has much to catch up on. But how can he do that? Who will take care of the boy?

(The conundrum gives birth to an idea for his novel *Mother Love*: he jots a note to himself—the boy will stay with Mother. Every hour she spends with the boy today will only make those hours and days she does not see him all the more painful in the future.)

With a twinge in his stomach, Kalich realizes the converse of his idea is also true. If he had the courage to open himself to love, intimacy, life, rather than deny himself, he would have had little inner necessity to create the novel *Mother Love* (or for that matter, *The Nihilesthete)* in the first place.

Kalich meets an old producer-friend who has attained virtually reverential status for having produced many of the theater world's most original playwrights. The producer called him two weeks past, saying he needed to talk. At lunch his friend tells him that he and his partner, whom he has lived with for thirty-four years and financed all his productions, have had a rift. Edward says,

I've done nothing important with my life. Producing plays is not important. Not unless they make money. And the playwrights and arthouse plays I've produced do not. Now in our old age, because of me, we have to worry about rent. Just surviving.

MAH NISHTANAH, HA-LALAH HA-ZEH MI KOL HA-LELOT.

What does that mean?

It means, said Kalich:

WHY SHOULD THIS NIGHT BE DIFFERENT THAN ANY OTHER NIGHT?

My father, the cantor, used to recite it every year at the Passover table.

Kalich is nearing the end of his book and, to be safe, decides to have it Xeroxed. He leaves the manuscript at the West 71st Street store with the copyist, Lee, whom he has known for virtually his entire writing life and who has proven to be an astute reader with sound critical judgment. The next day, Lee tells him, as is his custom, that he made an extra copy of the manuscript and took it home to read. He goes on to say that Kalich made a major conceptual mistake with the book.

In your novel *Penthouse F* you characterize yourself as fictional. But in this book, you establish the same character, the writer, Richard Kalich, as real from the start. In fact, you take pains to identify the book as a biographical narrative and yet you repeat many of the same incidents and life experiences as you depicted in the novel. I was confused at first. It's not like you to err in this way. Either your Richard Kalich is imagined as in *Penthouse F* or real, but the way you have it with this book it seems you want it both ways. All those readers who have read *Penthouse F* will spot this quickly.

Kalich doesn't answer the copyist. Doesn't give a hint of being perturbed. If anything, there's a bemused expression on his face. But once again, in this case with the copyist Lee, if not himself, there is confusion between fiction and reality. Art and life. And, of course, that is the challenge of this book. Can Kalich transcend the Mind-Body Split? Can he become Haberman? Even at this late stage—he still doesn't know. Only finishing the book will tell him.

He can only hope his readers are as anxious to know as he is.

Before leaving the Xerox store, he gives the copyist an unusually generous tip.

After having saved for several months, Kalich has sufficient money to purchase one of his very few indulgences for the year: Persol sunglasses.

At Barney's, the salesgirl who appears twenty-two tells him she's thirty-two and married. Surprised, Kalich asks: Any children?

No, the salesgirl answers, but I have a dog.

Again surprised, but this time at himself. Why should he feel such disdain, contempt even enmity towards this pleasant-enough young woman?

His mind drifts off to conjure Thomas Bernhard's excoriation of dog lovers. It bothers him a little that he cannot recall the title of the novel. But that is quickly offset by Bernhard's like-minded conviction to his own.

As we know, Kalich believes in the hierarchy of values. From the transcendence of art to dog lovers whom he has always thought of as maudlin. He's built his life on such values. Has his life been richer for it? Or made poorer by such thinking?

Kalich concludes, with the fall of the literary culture, the joke's on him. Is it any wonder he's writing the novel *Mother Love*?

In the early evening, the two young people at the Equinox front desk give him a quixotic look when he makes reference to a favorite book or author. Both college graduates and aspiring actors, Kalich is always disturbed that not only don't they read such classic novelists as Gide, Kafka, Mann, but they are not even familiar with their names.

Something similar can be said of Kalich's sixteen-year-old nephew, Knute. Though highly intelligent, he doesn't read fiction unless it's mandated in school.

It occurs to Kalich he has not read a novel in at least four months, not since he started writing *The Assisted Living Facility Library*.

That night, Kalich attends a jazz concert at Lincoln Center, featuring a mutual friend of his and the Harpist. As their friend is a renowned, innovative composer and pianist, he's drawn a young, enthusiastic, international audience. The Harpist's investor-husband has brought along a severe-looking woman, who Kalich has learned from the Harpist is among the most powerful people in the banking industry. When the woman asks him how he and Pia met, he explains, adding a smile, he had a long adolescence.

You know what they call that, the banker says.

And without waiting for Kalich's reply she answers her own question: Arrested Development.

Kalich was about to make a smart remark when the Harpist placed her hand on his knee.

Following the concert, they wait for the composer, but as he's swamped by a congratulatory mob and then becomes engaged in a seemingly endless conversation with a woman, both the investor and the banker become impatient. Tomorrow's a workday and, after asking Kalich to convey their regrets for not being able to stay and offer well wishes, they leave. Pia, who has to drive her two little girls to school early the next morning, reluctantly leaves too.

Finally, the artist breaks free. Apologizing profusely for the long wait, he excitedly tells Kalich that he attended a shiva the previous night for a woman he knew as a kid in Miami Beach, Florida. She had lived on Sutton

Place and all her friends from that area, he says, are miles ahead of the Central Park West people he and Kalich know as neighbors. The woman had a library even larger than Kalich's and she had the greatest collection of CD's. She was well-rounded. Not like Kalich. Really loved sophisticated music. That was her daughter he was speaking to just now. When she came up to him he didn't recognize her. An old bag. When she was nineteen he had a crush on her. And would've loved to bang her. Tonight, not only didn't he recognize her, but he couldn't wait to get away.

Before leaving his friend, Kalich confessed that amidst the hip, young, international crowd, he's the one who felt like an old bag.

Kalich hates the winter.

One false step and he could be on crutches with a broken hip, or worse, for months.

Home at last, Kalich is relieved to find he left his trundle bed unmade. It requires a great effort for him to get down on his hands and knees every night to pull out the trundle bed from underneath the sofa. From here on he resolves not to make his bed. At least on the weekdays. That will save him from wasting valuable strength and energy. Besides, the last thing he wants is to have anyone visit his apartment and see Mother and the boy.

About to close his eyes to sleep, he notices a dust ball on the floor.

Always something.

He can still hear his twin yelling upon entering his penthouse apartment: Your apartment is filthy!

And he was right. There were always dust balls underneath the trundle bed and on occasion, not all the time, even spiderwebs hanging from the ceiling. When it came to his own apartment, his twin was scrupulously clean and neat. Going so far as to employ a cleaning lady two times a week, even when he couldn't afford it.

And yet, between the two, it was Kalich who was the dandy. He recalls when they were in their early twenties discovering Jimmy Carroll's Men's Boutique on Madison Avenue. When he came home with a three hundred-dollar sport jacket his brother let out a tirade: What are you crazy?! How could you spend $300 on a sport jacket?

A month later, his brother had two Jimmy Carroll sport

jackets hanging in his own closet as well as a suit.

After hearing his last composed pages, Kalich's young neighbor, whom he has regularly read his work to as he progressed, said he should concentrate more on the fiction, *Mother Love*, and the violence perpetrated on Mother and the boy by Haberman. Kalich agrees: that will only help center the entire work, and in today's world plot and conflict are everything. He promises himself on the second draft he will give more time and effort to Mother's punishing sequences.

The question remains: not will he, but at this age, can he do it?

The partners are in perfect unison. Before the words are out of one partner's mouth, the other one knows exactly what he has in mind. It's as if they are attending a séance, and the medium is passing mystic secrets onto them from above. It is impossible to tell which of the two has given birth to an original idea. To say that their battle plan originated from one or the other would be unfair to both.

The partners set to work immediately implementing their plan. Mother's space is completely overhauled. From a barren and empty space every indulgence is made available to Mother. No expense is too great. No cost too high. Kalich has put aside a contingency fund for just such purposes. Whatever her taste buds desire: rustic; modern; futuristic; traditional—she will have.

Carpenters; electricians; wood craftsmen; avant-garde furniture designers busy themselves non-stop around the clock. The four walls and floor are redone. The ceiling is speckled with shooting stars. A handyman builds a custom-made doghouse as Kalich thought it a good idea that the boy have a pet. And on the very same day Haberman brings home a stray little Maltese. By the end of the week

Mother's space has the appearance of a regal chamber; her once rickety, wooden crate chair seems like a throne seat.

With the room's renovation complete, a renowned fashion consultant is called in and with the aid of the furniture designer and a handyman, Mother's toss-on-the-floor bag lady's pile is transformed into the most elegant wardrobe closet and 18th century French armoire. Mother's emaciated, shaking frame, once covered in a raggedy, tattered blanket, is clothed from stem to stern in fabrics of the finest quality: satin, silk, damask, vicuna, cashmere. Dozens of shoes lie at her feet. Necklaces, bracelets, rings, Tiffany's and Harry Winston jewelry adorn her every body part.

For breakfast, lunch, and dinner Mother selects from time-tested recipes by internationally acclaimed award-winning chefs who made their culinary mark preparing exotic foods for the most discerning palates at five-star restaurants. On special occasions—such as Christmas; Hanukkah; birthdays; Bar Mitzvahs; Confirmations—the partners employ added help: busboys and waiters; but for the quotidian everyday—school days, 9-5 workdays—the partners dressed in livery serving the three meals suffice. Additionally, a full-time maître d' dressed in a tuxedo is at Mother's beck and call.

Overnight, Mother's life has gone from deprivation and

hardship to the lap of luxury.

Meanwhile, the boy continues to reside in an isolated corner of Kalich's modest room. And that is the partners' plan. To fatten Mother for the slaughter and then have her choose between her present good fortune and the boy. She can have one or the other—but not both. The partners wait with bated breath to see which Mother, of her own volition, will choose.

Despite, as always, standing at half-mast and remaining mute and dead-eyed, Mother instantly chooses the boy.

With all the time, care, and cost the partners have invested, they are disappointed.

But not defeated.

Indeed, they relish the challenge.

Perhaps, the next plan will show different results.

And there will be a next plan.

And they will be there to see it.

Later that week, Kalich's brother called him from his second home in North Salem. He tells Kalich he spent the whole day, from 7:30 in the morning to 3:30 this afternoon, reading his new novel. He agrees with him. He didn't realize it when he was writing it, but it is his best book. Kalich is excited and is about to tell his twin how he's finally realized all his talents; how this book is not only his best book yet, but one of the best novels he's read in years, when his brother interrupts him saying Knute just walked over. Say hello. Kalich is upset. No, angry. He doesn't want to talk to the sixteen-year-old, he wants to talk to his brother about his book.

The next morning his brother calls again: What did you say to Knute?! Don't you realize you're eighty years old. He doesn't want to hear about your book or your opinion that any moron can make money. There's a whole world separating us from him today.

Kalich hung up.

Hours later, though he's had time to digest his brother's words, he's still angry.

A full day later?

—the same.

First and foremost, dress Mother for the occasion. A flimsy filigree night dress will do. Let Mother kiss, hold, hug, and caress the boy for a minute. Two. As long as she wants. Then, when she least expects it, remove the boy from her grasp. Vary the intervals of Mother's caresses from one hour to nothing at all. Continue the game to your heart's content. Just make certain that before you withhold the boy, Mother is in a state of maternal bliss; and, conversely, that she is hungering for the next allotment before you grant the boy again. The most essential point is to keep Mother off guard; not knowing when the boy will be bestowed. Somewhere between expectancy and denial at once. And always cognizant that no matter how plentiful the hugs and kisses are in one moment, they can be taken away the next.

For no reason at all.

There is no way for Mother to prepare a defense; to gauge the intervals of the boy's affections. Mother resides someplace between heaven and hell. She is at the mercy of the Gods.

Cruel Gods whose Rules of the Game are not hers to discern.

Such is the game Kalich and Haberman are playing.

Like a fly buzzing around one's nose, when one brushes one nostril, it goes to the other. No matter how many flicks of the wrist, the fly returns or doesn't of its own accord. Until one gives up altogether. For sure, it's never up to the one flicking one's wrist; it is always up to the fly.

This game can go on for as long as one wants. Mother has no say in the matter. But, still, what's more interesting than anything else is that Mother never yields. Never ceases to participate in the game. Never gives up hope that sooner or later her luck will change, and the boy will stay forever. And if not forever, another second or minute will do just fine. For a second or a minute of such bliss must seem like forever to one as famished as Mother.

But, of course, there is no real certainty to any of this. Mother lives in a state of incredulity—false hope; maybe this time, maybe not; forever and never. Will the boy return, or won't he? Everything given can be taken away; every kindness is only on loan; at the whim and fancy of the Other.

Finally, it's not so much that Mother yields as the game loses its appeal. The partners grow tired of it. They move on to another game.

Still, they are more than satisfied. Mother has proven herself to be a formidable opponent. Certainly deserving of more of the same.

For the first time, Kalich feels the punishments meted out to Mother this afternoon were every bit as dark, perverse, and cruel as the ones he had Haberman dole out to Brodski in his novel, *The Nihilesthete*. And much of it was of his own initiative. Not Haberman's.

One can never be certain how the unconscious works, but Kalich thinks it has something to do with having dinner the previous night with The Harpist, her investor husband, and two young daughters. The girls are complete opposites: Yvette, loving, outgoing, and wholly expectant of the world's smiles; Thea, contemplative, quiet, hesitant. They have been like that since birth. Also, and no small thing—Pia was miserable all evening. Even sobbing on the phone when she called Kalich the next morning. Her problem is and has always been the same. She has nothing in common with her husband. Visiting Manhattan for the weekend on one of their rare getaways from Greenwich, she had looked forward for weeks to visiting a museum, art gallery, the theater with her husband and kids as a family. Instead, he insisted on taking the girls to a *Star Wars* movie and shopping.

What did she know when she was young from Bulgaria about choosing a husband?

And finally, the coup de grâce. Purchase a large block of ice sufficient in size to equal the width and breadth of Mother's seat. Make use of an old rocking chair in Kalich's apartment. Position the ice directly beneath her rump. Lay the boy gently on her lap with her arms preternaturally folded around him. Cover her torso and chest so that the cold cannot reach the boy. Encourage her, not that she needs encouragement, to rock back and forth, to and fro, in the ancient rhythm mothers have done since the beginning of time. But she cannot stand up. She cannot leave her post. If she so much as lifts herself an inch from the chair, no matter how cold, no matter how much she squirms, wriggles, does all she can to insulate herself from the cold, her playdate is over. The game is finished. The boy will promptly be removed from her embrace and returned to Kalich's room.

Mother is permitted to hug, squeeze, cuddle, kiss, hold, rock to and fro, back and forth, but she is not permitted to raise herself one inch from the chair.

Vary the playdate by exchanging the rocking chair and block of ice for a love seat and a radiator or portable elec-

tric heater laser-focused on—you guessed it—Mother's rump. If you prefer, a hot plate or even glowing hot coals gathered from the fireplace or basement furnace—it's up to you. Use your imagination. There are plenty of variations on this theme. In regular intervals, increase the heat from lukewarm to hot to burning flame. You will find that Mother is so orgiastically lost in her need for the boy's love that she is oblivious to the impending danger. That is until she can't help but notice the smoking fumes from the love seat and the stench of her own burning flesh.

No doubt, you will savor the moment, but don't fail to take notice of Mother closing her eyes shut; squirming in her seat; clenching her teeth; grimacing and contorting her torso and sundry other frantic gestures she might call upon to relieve the heat. And even if she is not conscious of the danger, you are—to be sure, it will only increase your spectator's joy and thrill. And rest assured, Mother won't give up her seat. After all, the boy is the star of stars, the object of her affection, and, of course, the show must go on.

Yet, please be aware this game is not without a caveat. With all the smoke and smell of burning flesh the neighbors just might take it upon themselves to call "New York's Bravest" to the rescue.

It is a known fact that smoke clouds from concentration

camp furnaces could be seen by villagers for miles around.

If Mother is asked to choose between the block of ice and hot seat, one can only wonder which she would select.

When she was asked to make just such a choice—she could not. She just sat frozen, staring her dead-eyed stare. Not once was she able to muster sufficient will to make a choice.

Yet, one had the distinct impression that everything inside her wanted to move; ached to do something more.

Kalich is nearly embarrassed to admit this, but he got the idea for the block of ice and hot seat from visiting a lifelong friend at the hospital, suffering from an inoperable brain tumor diagnosed as terminal. When Kalich entered the room his friend instantly leapt from his chair and hugged him as if hanging on for dear life. Kalich had never been crushed so hard in his life. Such is the way Mother must have understood the nature of the game; the irregularity and unpredictability of time allotments. For she, too, crushed the boy in ostensibly last gasp hugs as if hanging on for dear life.

Once again, something deep inside Kalich is stirring. A push and pull. An inner stirring.

This time Kalich knows what it means. What he has to do.

First and foremost, Kalich has to free himself from Haberman. He has to go on this journey alone—with Mother and the boy. If he's to truly test his limits, explore all his possibilities, Kalich has to break his bond with his character, Haberman, with the fictions he's created; he has to stand alone.

Kalich is on the precipice of self-discovery. Of becoming more than he is. Becoming that which up to now he has only been able to imagine and write about.

But this is no longer merely writing.

And Kalich is no longer merely a writer.

This is life. Kalich's life.

Testing his limits, exploring his possibilities, uniting and coalescing the two sides of himself, mind and body, inner and outer, in his struggle to become whole is what Kalich has been working towards all this time. And just as Kalich trashed his books, he must now trash Mother and the boy. He must let go of them as fictional representations and see them for who they are: People.

In order to achieve what he has envisioned from the start, Kalich must become Haberman—not in words, but in deeds. Not in his mind, but in his life.

On Sunday, the three will go to Central Park. Kalich knows an area in the park, The Ramble, where homeless people as well as homosexuals congregate. He is well aware that it is dangerous there. That anything can happen there. Murder, rape, all sorts of mayhem and chaos.

The Ramble should serve as an ideal place for Kalich to enact his plan.

That night, Kalich commenced making preparations for the trek to The Ramble.

All Kalich has to do is fill his backpack with a first-aid kit, matches, water, flashlight, pocket knife, extra sweaters, and blankets. Additionally, he will carry a walking stick and perhaps an umbrella and several ponchos in case of rain.

His refrigerator is already well-stocked with peanut butter and jelly sandwiches—the boy's favorite. Mother's too. As for himself, Kalich's doctor has advised him that at his age, eating an apple daily (with the skin) will help with his constipation and whole wheat bread is preferable to rye or white.

Kalich knows the trek will not be easy. (At his age, nothing is.) And he is more than a little concerned about his strength and stamina.

But not nearly as much as about the sole purpose for the journey. To imagine dastardly deeds is one thing; to commit the deeds oneself—that is a different story altogether.

However, that is what is required if Kalich is to learn once and for all if he can live his art in life.

Wearing heavy walking boots, which he purchased only last week, Kalich, Mother, and the boy left his apartment early Sunday morning. Kalich was pleased that there were no residents in the lobby to ask meddling questions and that the doorman was engaged in a heated conversation with the weekend concierge and neither looked up. Mother and the boy were in a particularly jovial mood. It was as if they were anticipating some sort of adventure. And though Kalich's demeanor is never readily discernible, it seemed as if he were starting a new novel.

Or—as if he were looking forward to the trek like a rite of passage.

Before Kalich headed directly to The Ramble, he decided to give the boy and Mother a genuine send-off. Something comparable to a prisoner's last meal; and he made a stopover at the Hill on West 73rd Street, in front of the Lake where the Guitar Man of Central Park performs during spring, summer, and fall months. Even though a crowd of 150 to 200 sit on the knoll regularly, there's always room for a few more to find seating space on the grass and spend a delightful hour or two listening to his pop renditions.

The view from the Hill overlooking the Lake and Woods is among the most beautiful vistas in Central Park.

And as the Oak Bridge spanning Bay Rock Bay in the Lake's northwest corner is the major entrance to The Ramble from the westside, it is only a few minutes' walk to the Hill.

As we know, saving strength and energy is always a consideration for Kalich.

What impressed Kalich most before leaving the Hill

was not so much that he didn't enjoy the music, he did, even if his mind was weighed down with other concerns, but Mother and the boy. Particularly, the way the pair responded to the Guitar Man's music.

The boy instantly leapt up from his grass seat, bounded down the hill, stopping directly in front of the singer. Whereupon, he commenced dancing—if one can call his awkward movements and childlike gyrations dancing. All smiles, the Guitar Man accompanied the boy with his music and encouraged him with banter. It was a moment so pure, so filled with innocence and good feeling, that the people on the hill responded in kind with shouts and hurrahs, spurring the boy to even greater frenzy. And sooner than not, joined in by clapping in rhythm to the boy's frenzied steps.

But what impressed Kalich even more than the boy's dancing was Mother's response. Whether it was the music, the crowd, the greenery, Mother's broken body became at ease. No longer shaking or bent over at half mast, Mother's body becalmed, composed itself, and she also began swaying to the rhythm of the music.

She even smiled at Kalich when she caught him staring at her.

Kalich carried the boy's dancing and Mother's smile with him after they left the Hill and for a goodly portion of their trek through The Ramble.

By the time Kalich, Mother, and the boy set off it was already late afternoon. Kalich had engaged the Guitar Man in conversation and was surprised to learn that he had been homeless as a youth and was somewhat familiar with Mother's background as well. But that was long ago, and as much as Kalich probed and delved, the Guitar Man wouldn't reveal more.

As soon as they made their way from the bridge to The Ramble, in contrast to the halcyon setting of the Hill, though artificially made, the Woods jarred Kalich to the core. By comparison, Mother and the boy remained calm and tranquil and had little or no difficulty with the change. Kalich, on the other hand, stumbled about. The winding paths and dense clumps of tree trunks were not at all smooth, some not even accessible. Kalich was instantly fearful of falling, his balance was not what it once had been, and he began breathing heavily almost immediately.

From atop an embankment, though rapidly getting dark, Kalich was able to gain a sense of the immense vastness of the wooded area. Thanks to the Guitar

Man's instructions and pencil-sketched map, Kalich had a vague sense of where he was headed, but every five or ten minutes he would stop not only to catch his breath, his heart racing each and every time he trespassed a steep incline, but to listen to the birds. He was astounded by the beauty of the bird song that was all the more beautiful because of the great variety of birds that remained hidden amidst the trees, shrubbery, and bushes.

Now and again Kalich gained a glimmer of city light. Whether it was Central Park South or West he didn't know, but the very fact that he was amidst something familiar gave him enormous comfort. On the other hand, Mother and the boy hardly noticed, seeming to become more comfortable in the woods with each passing stride.

Even the sight of a raccoon or two didn't disrupt their progress, but when an entire troop of at least fifteen to twenty raccoons marched diagonally across their path, the boy stopped, laughed, and pointing his finger, yelped with joy: Look, Momma, they're like a little army of soldiers.

For the second time that day, Mother smiled not only at the boy, but at Kalich too.

tial downpour.

Mother and the boy journeyed on, every now and then stopping to wait for Kalich to catch up. Without once availing themselves of the map, Kalich was all the more convinced they knew where they were going.

All at once, more than a little beyond their view, were the faintest sounds of music, voices, animals, something. Kalich could not tell what. But it was there. At least he thought he heard something. But when he stopped, despite his wobbly legs, and climbed atop a rocky outcrop of glacially-scarred Manhattan bedrock, he could not see anything other than the usual shadowy trees and wooded area. Because his legs would not support him, he had to crawl back on his hands and knees.

Perhaps, it was the birdsong. Perhaps, he was imagining things.

It would not be the first time.

Or the last.

Mother and the boy gave no indication of anything out of the ordinary.

Because of the rain and despite following the Guitar Man's map, progress was slow. Kalich wouldn't allow himself to be hurried by Mother and the boy's quickened pace on what was now not merely a slipshod and watery path, but perilous. Indeed, Kalich was obliged to stop in ever more frequent intervals, and not only to catch his breath, but to rub his arms and legs in a vain attempt to get back his circulation. Without these constant breaks, it would have been impossible for him to continue.

But, of course, he was resolved to do so. He had not come this far to give up now.

Not when so much was at stake.

Mother and the boy continued to wait patiently for him to catch up before trekking on.

Kalich was repeatedly amazed at how only the smallest rest would revitalize him, allowing him to march on with renewed vigor and energy.

Kalich didn't have to shout protestations about being old. Disdain for his decrepitude poured out of every muffled utterance and with every bodily gesture.

And all this decrepitude, in spite of working out at Equinox for at least an hour three times a week.

He could only imagine what he'd be without such exercise.

In the distance was a light flickering. As they moved closer, still remaining hidden, Kalich and Mother could make out four or five spectral figures hunched over an oil drum lit with flame. Wine or beer bottles in their hands. Kalich could not discern their features, but by the way they were moving or dancing, they were definitely crazed, drunk, or high on one drug or another. It was dark. Silent. Mother moved to hide the boy behind the shrubbery. One of the men spotted her, pointing his hand. There was nowhere to run or hide. Through the blackness the men commenced to move towards them.

Kalich stood stock-still. This was his moment. What would he do? Could he do what he had come for? Would he be able to abandon Mother and the boy to their fate as he had thought and planned for so long?

The sky was black and stagnant. No moon or stars above. Still, the tiniest glow from the city continued to irradiate from afar; as if from the depths rather than the sky. There was an aura of viscous stillness as the four men with no recognizable features moved towards them like a pack of hunting animals towards their prey.

As they approached, their shadowy figures appeared to grow larger, as if large, viscous, and silent enough to take up the whole night. That's all there was—these dark, lifeless, gigantic figures coming closer and closer.

Kalich remained frozen.

Suddenly, Mother stepped forward. Handing the boy to Kalich, she pointed towards an escape route. Without saying a word, Mother moved away from Kalich and the boy, towards the homeless men.

Carrying the boy in his arms, Kalich reached home in the wee hours. He was upset that he had to wake the concierge to open the door as he had nodded off.

Neither Kalich nor the boy had enough strength to do anything but fall into bed and sleep.

Upon awakening the following afternoon, the first thing Kalich noticed was that the apartment appeared enormous. Evidently, while he was gone, the Building Manager had taken it upon himself (with the aid of several porters) to empty the apartment of trashed books.

That was certainly his custom: Whenever an old resident died or, as in Kalich's case, was scheduled to enter an Assisted Living Facility or a nursing home, he and the senior handyman, John C, would scavenge the vacated apartment for anything remaining of value: a first edition or a signed copy by a famous writer was always worth something, even in today's world.

Kalich had more important things on his mind. In addition to his aching limbs, every muscle and joint in his body hurt in one way or another, the boy needed attending to. He had not had a bath since they left for The Ramble, nor had he eaten anything since the peanut butter and jelly sandwich at least twenty-four hours earlier.

Fortunately, Kalich's refrigerator remains well-stocked.

Still, in his entire life, Kalich had never given a child a bath and, though reluctant and feeling awkward, he mustered his courage to do so now. The warm water, suds, and, especially, the manner by which the boy surrendered his body to his touch was an entirely new and pleasing experience for Kalich.

Lunch proved equally satisfying. Not merely the usual peanut butter and jelly sandwiches, but a real feast. Chocolate pudding followed by a tomato salad, centered by canned salmon.

After lunch, the boy helped Kalich with the dishes.

Peculiarly, the boy has not once made mention of Mother.

Kalich's young neighbor visited him in the late afternoon. After offering his sympathies again to Kalich for not realizing his quest, he reports on Kalich's first foray into describing The Ramble incident. Though he's never truly understood Kalich's quest, or for that matter, the dynamic between Kalich, Haberman, and Mother, this latest rendering left him wholly unsatisfied. It still sounds like it's more in the writer's mind than real, more about art than life. The payoff for the reader isn't fully there.

The young man's response catches Kalich off guard. In defensive tones, Kalich explains that though he's at a loss as to what to do about the boy, with the book not so much. Just like life intervened with his quest at The Ramble, he can free himself from Haberman not by becoming Haberman, but by letting him go.

Interesting idea, says the youth. Follow it. See where it takes you. And not only in your mind, but with your body, too, he smiles.

That night in bed Kalich is surprised to feel he has no regrets. All those years he's spent conjuring Haberman have not been wasted.

Despite his years, Kalich sleeps well that night.

When Kalich wakes the next morning, he understands...

—what is important now is to decide what to do with the boy.

Not every hour of the day has to be devoted to the boy. By nightfall the boy will be asleep. Then Kalich can do with the hours what he wants. Read a book. Watch television. Relax.

Somehow relaxing in front of the TV doesn't seem as appealing now. Nor does reading ten pages or more a day seem necessary any longer.

The world is different today than it was yesterday or has

been since time immemorial.

Of that Kalich is certain.

A new and added difference is the boy.

All Kalich's life everything seemed important.

Too important.

Not now.

No longer.

What you accomplished as a writer is great. But it's still only half-a-life.

His twin said that—more than once.

Many, many times.

Kalich still takes comfort in perusing his one hundred Favorite Books. He knows each and every title so well. Some might regard books as old friends. Kalich has always disdained that kind of sentimentality. Yet, he does receive satisfaction, an inner nourishment, just viewing the bookshelves. Just knowing the books are there.

Still....

Before he died, the Israeli's lover, "Everybody's Best Friend," Abe, said to the twins: Don't feel sorry for me, boys. In my seventy years, I've lived seven hundred.

On the other hand, Kalich repeatedly asks himself: How many years has he lived? Really lived?

His novel *Charlie P* is about a man who lived his life by not living it.

And, though a parabolic tale, *Charlie P* is as much memoir as fiction.

All those books read, annotated, studied, underlined in two, three, four different colored pencils. Read, reread. And reread again.

Now, just envisioning all those books in his mind, brings upon Kalich a profound lassitude. Makes him sad.

Kalich wonders... what does it all mean?

What?!

What Kalich knows, nobody knows. What everybody knows, Kalich does not.

The past several days, Kalich has read the paper every morning and watched the TV news every night. Not once has he heard anything mentioned about an incident in The Ramble.

Nothing about Mother and four homeless men.

This might seem peculiar to some, but, personally, Kalich held no animosity towards Mother. There's no need for labels here. Kalich wanted to turn fiction to reality; to enact his fictional incarnation of evil, Haberman, by exploring the possibility of MIND (the real, his biographical narrative, *The Assisted Living Facility Library*) and BODY (the imagined, his novel, *Mother Love*) becoming one. Not in the abstract, not merely with words, but in flesh and blood reality. But, as stated, now that the exploration is over, he holds no grudges. On the contrary, he only hopes that a day comes soon when the concierge will announce Mother on the intercom and she'll walk through the door ready to resume residence with him and the boy once more.

Kalich can't help himself and scours the apartment for

any stray and overlooked books left behind. His search proves fruitful. He finds underneath the bottom shelf of his book-closet Kafka's diary, *I am a Memory Come Alive.* He can't leave this volume behind. Not only is it his favorite Kafka, it's one of the most significant autobiographical achievements in literary history.

But nooooo. Kalich catches himself. He's reverting to type. He has responsibilities to attend to. The boy requires care, constant attention.

Books for now, even Kafka's, are definitely not as important any longer.

Recognizing this last thought makes Mother's sacrifice more palatable for Kalich.

Still, he does not sleep any better than the boy who continues to twist and turn in his sleep.

Nothing in the papers again this morning about a homeless woman assaulted, raped, murdered in The Ramble.

Nothing about four homeless men either.

Waking this morning, Kalich remembers he has yet to

call Social Services, but sooner or later he must.

If memory doesn't fail him, he is scheduled to be admitted to the Assisted Living Facility at the end of the month, the last Thursday, if not mistaken. He has the date written in Sharpie pen bold letters in his annual calendar book on his desk.

By then, he should be fully recovered from his aches and pains.

But what about the boy?

He has yet to decide what to do about the boy.

Actually, Kalich has already discussed the matter with the Facility Director, Mrs. Longua, who, in turn, referred him to her friend at Social Services. So, all that is required is a phone call.

So why has he not yet made the call?

Also, Mrs. Longua said she would send someone over to collect his one hundred favorite books. So, all things considered, matters are pretty much in hand.

All that remains is for Kalich to decide what to do with

the boy.

And not even that.

He just has to make the call.

Speaking of the boy, Kalich's refrigerator is well-stocked: besides peanut butter and jelly sandwiches, and two loaves of white bread (one whole-wheat for himself), he has:

* Kashi GoLean Cereal Honey Almond Flax
* Kind Healthy Grains (oats and honey clusters)
* Kind Healthy Grains (banana nuts clusters)
* Bite 4 Bite Love Crunch (apple chia crumble)
* Banana Nut Clusters (the boy seems partial to these)
* Orange and Pineapple juice
* Fresh fruit: peaches, pears, bananas, (apples for
    himself)

Additionally, he has an assortment of meats in the freezer.

For the next week or two, food is his least worry.

Still, what he doesn't have and will have to go shopping for is milk. He had no idea how much milk a little squirt like the boy would consume. Milk for breakfast; milk for lunch; milk for dinner; not to mention snacks and something chocolaty with milk at the end of the day before sleep.

Two or three large one gallon Farmland fat-free containers should do the trick.

Do children require vitamins?

He'll have to ask the handyman; he and his wife have a little boy just about the boy's age.

It's not easy being a father. Imagine how difficult it must be for a homeless woman.

Perhaps instead of making repeated trips to the grocery each time, he can have one of the building staff shop for him. He must remember to ask the building manager which of the staff would make a suitable candidate. Fortunately, he has always been on good terms with the building manager. The man respects his being a writer more than most people in today's world.

And why not? He's Irish—the last remnants of an Irish poet.

Though he is taking one hundred books to the Facility, one sturdy youth should be able to manage.

He must remember to replace Salinger's *The Catcher in the Rye* for Kafka's *I am a Memory Come Alive.*

There is another possibility. One of the four homeless men is the boy's father, Mother's husband, friend, lover, mate. If so, perhaps Mother chose to stay in The Ramble with him of her own accord.

It would not be the first time a Mother sacrificed herself to give her child a better life.

His telephone doesn't stop ringing. Probably his twin, whom he has yet to bring up-to-date on the boy, Mother, and especially the trek to The Ramble.

Still, he must know something's going on.

He always does.

Needless to say, Kalich will continue working on his novel once he's settled in at the Facility. As for the boy...

...he still hasn't decided about the boy.

But that's his own affair.

His brother has his own novel to write.

Miraculously, though it might have taken him all his life to do so, he's finally mastered the craft and can write his novel without help from Kalich.

As arranged, a young man from the Assisted Living Facility came this morning to collect Kalich's books. Though familiar with several of the authors' names, he had not read any of the books. It's not his thing, he said. Reading's hard. He's into running. He ran the marathon last year.

The apartment looks more enormous than ever.

If not for the boy, empty.

There is a great difference between Kalich's growing attachment to the boy and his original vision for the book. Neither *The Assisted Living Facility Library* nor *Mother Love* did he want to title it, but *Protoplasm*. A photo he took at his brother's father-in-law's ranch in Chicota, Texas, of a cow's entrails eaten away by coyotes and vultures he had in mind to use as a book jacket to metaphorically depict his vision of the world.

That was then: this is now:

Kalich had no idea how his book would turn out until his trek to The Ramble.

As his twin has always said: Every sentence he writes is a surprise.

It seems—the same can be said of Kalich.

It all seems so unimportant now. His writing. Books. Reading ten pages or more a day. Tonight, he has to bathe and feed the boy. Put him to bed. That's important. The rest—not so much.

The boy is constantly sad. His eyes always moist. He continues to twist and turn in his sleep. The boy takes up all his time. If only Mother were here to help, but she's not. It is solely up to him to do what has to be done.

The boy has no one, but him.

Even if the boy cannot articulate it in words, Kalich wonders if on a deeper, more primal level, the boy can understand Mother Love.

Mother Love is the foundation stone and core basis of everything in life.

The ontic ballast of faith, trust, love, expectancy, hope—

The prerequisite conduit to the Human Heart—

This is why Kalich chose to take Mother into his life and make her the basis of his work in the first place.

Little good does his book do him or the boy now.

No different than the boy, Kalich continues to twist and turn in his sleep.

Whatever possessed him to write such a book? Live such a life? Test his limits? Become Haberman!?

It's been nearly two weeks, and still the papers and TV news have not mentioned a word about Mother. It's as if she never was.

Then again, why should they?—a single homeless person.

It's like the entire literary culture has no place in the world today. All his concerns. Values, his life. Everything he believed in.

—The Word.

—Depth.

—Interiority.

—The Self.

—The irreducible value of a single Human Being.

—Nothing sacred. Nothing holy.

For every "yes" he received over a lifetime, he received a hundred "no's."

Thousands of unanswered phone calls. Rejections.

Was it worth it?

For what?!

Art versus life. Kalich chose art.

He didn't even have a say in the matter.

Not really.

If only he did. He would have... should have...

To choose a book over life. A life. Any life.

Of course, he chose a book.

A great book.

Dostoevsky. Mann. Kafka.

Would he do it today? Now? Again?

He chose a book—to write one book that belongs on the shelf rather than to live a life.

A whole life.

A complete life.

His life.

His novel *Charlie P* was about a man who lived his life by not living it.

Charlie P was as much memoir as fiction.

Does it belong on the shelf? Even if it does...

Would he do it differently today if he could?

Maybe.

Maybe he can. If not for himself, for the boy.

What good is a book if there is no one to read it? Today nobody reads. The literary culture is dead. So over. There is an absence of beauty in the world. In his life. All his books have been trashed. Even his favorite one hundred books have been carted away. But not—not the boy.

Not yet.

There is still the boy who twists and turns with moist reddened eyes, mouthing like a recitativo unintelligible words in his sleep. The boy is still here. By placing his ear close to the boy's lips, like playing unintelligible words over and over again on his telephone answering machine, Kalich is able to piece together the boy's words: I want my Mommy. I want my Mommy.

There is such pain and sorrow, a great sorrow on the boy's face.

But he is still here.

The boy is still here.

One would have to be blind not to see such sorrow. One would have to be catatonic not to feel the boy's pain.

Kalich is not blind.

Kalich is not catatonic.

When asked to babysit for Knute, he would count the minutes until his brother and wife returned to their apartment.

He had more important things to do.

What has Knute got to do with my life, he would say over and over again to his twin each and every time he babysat.

He believed it.

Now he doesn't.

Kalich is not blind.

Kalich is not catatonic.

But can he continue to change? Can he continue to grow? Can he continue to become more than he is? Or was?

These are the thoughts he thinks while the boy continues to twist and turn and mutter unintelligible words in his sleep.

His body no longer hurts. He has no more aches and pains. But deep inside him there is a sorrow so deep that he knows no book can heal it.

His twin brother's happiest moments were those mornings riding in the car for twenty minutes, taking Knute to school. And talking. Really talking.

All these years and he has not known such a moment.

Not since he was with the Israeli, when young, a boy himself. And that lasted for two months only.

With The Harpist, it was all in his mind.

Kalich has slept alone in his bed all his life.

Several years ago he told the Israeli, whom he calls once a year on July 29th, the day of their anniversary, that he has always slept alone, she turned silent. Speechless. She could not say a word.

Even though on the phone he knew she was crying.

At the time he laughed. Made light of it.

But not now.

Now...

He did not tell her how he has never been the same since being with her.

That was more than fifty years ago.

All his life, his twin has always been with a woman, until he reached the age of sixty-two. None for more than five years at a time. He has twice been married. Not him. Not Kalich. Kalich has been alone his whole life.

Regarding his writing, his twin always said: If one of us makes it as a writer, that's enough.

He meant it.

When *The Nihilesthete* was published and subsequently praised by the literati, his brother was happy for him. Satisfied.

Sometimes that is the way with twins.

Not so for Kalich. He could never have been so selfless. Of course, he didn't always have a woman in his life; and for the last seventeen years, Knute.

Kalich has not told the Building Manager or any of the building staff when he is entering the Assisted Living Facility.

Imagine, at this age, he is still capable of moral embarrassment. That is not a bad thing, he reflects. In today's world most don't even have that.

Only his twin brother and his brother's wife and Knute

know. Not one neighbor. Not any of his friends. At any rate, not any of those few friends still left.

The boy's nightmare wakes Kalich in the middle of the night. Tears are streaming down his cheeks. His features are twisted into a grotesque, heart-rending, hall-of-mirrors grimace.

Kalich carries the boy to his bed.

He would have made a good father, he thinks. The boy, a loving son.

As Pia has said so many times about her own daughters: Children are so easy to love.

For the rest of the night he holds the boy's thumb.

As much as he ever has, Kalich feels connected to the world.

The Assisted Living Facility proved to be a welcoming tonic for Kalich. The Director had made the author's four novels available at the Facility's library and a small but steady stream of residents could be seen making their way to the library each and every morning for at least the first several months. Much to his surprise, Kalich responded enthusiastically to his newfound celebrity. He had never before seen a book of his being read by an absolute stranger, and it was enough to lighten his usual dour mood.

But sooner than not, three months, no more, Kalich noticed interest waning and the residents beginning to peruse his pages with the same careless speed one scans the web today. Of course, there was always the exception. But for those who did take an interest, or at least seemed to, it wasn't so much for the literary merits of his novels; nor were they particularly curious about what the author had to say; or even how well he said it. Actually, what interested the residents was no different than what has always interested readers: a good story, a page-turner, and whether Kalich's novels were high art or pop art, fiction or biography, had little bearing on their selection.

As the years passed Kalich came to believe that is the way it should be. No longer did his books have to be prize winners. No longer did they have to be seminal works, like a Kafka or Beckett. There was no more comparison shopping for Kalich. No more questioning where he ranked amongst the world's greatest.

All those years of creative block, terror of art, terror of life, all those grandiose ambitions and grand illusions that plagued and burdened him all his life seem to him now—

H'enorme, Balzac said, the stupidity of mankind. H'enorme.

(Or was it Flaubert?)

What we do to ourselves nobody can do to us—(who said that?)

All his angst and anxiety. What does it mean now— Success/Failure; Self/World; Mind/Body; what do they mean now—here at the Assisted Living Facility?

Kalich does not even need Readers—not that he ever

had that many.

Kalich is finally content with who he is and not what he might become.

In the end, whether high art or pop art, imagined or real, writing filled up his life; made the hours pass fast; and most importantly, invested his life with indeterminate purport and meaning.

Oft times, when writing in the morning and editing his work in the afternoon, the hours flew by so fast that when he stopped for a minute to turn on the lights in his apartment to be able to continue writing, or just to read his scribblings, he was amazed to see that it was already dark outside.

Later, alone in his bed, he would ask himself, and not with words, wordlessly—what does it all mean?

What difference did all his reading and writing make?

What does he know today that he didn't know before?

His twin brother's words would resonate at those times: It's great what you accomplished as a writer, but it's still only half-a-life.

Kalich continues to read his ten pages or more a day. He never seems to tire of his books. A good book is like Man himself, he says: unknowable. And no matter how many times he reads a book, there is always something new to be found. It's as if with each reading something opens inside him and whether it's a word, an image, a keen insight, a well-turned phrase, he surrenders himself to its beauty and lets it in.

But more than anything at the Assisted Living Facility, Kalich looks forward to Sunday when the boy visits him. Though the boy has little predilection for reading, especially fiction, he heads a team in his middle school, constructing scale model computer-generated robots, which only recently won a competition in the New York and Connecticut areas. In fact, when he visits today he's scheduled to teach those residents who want to learn about the computer as well.

And so, whether Kalich has another day left or ten years at the Facility, he knows, like all his other days, it will start by his reading ten or more pages and then continue by working on his novel-in-progress. The only difference from earlier days is that now when Kalich hears a songbird chirping on his window's ledge, he stops to listen.

That same Sunday morning, a homeless woman visited the Facility; a tattered rag blanket partially covering her emaciated frame. Though she did not ask to speak to Kalich, she did leave a package for him and the boy. A few hours later, at noontime, when Kalich opened the package he found two peanut butter and jelly sandwiches—one white bread, the other whole-wheat.

The package additionally contained an apple.

Written August 15, 2017 – September 18, 2018
New York City

GREEN INTEGER
Pataphysics and Pedantry
Douglas Messerli, *Publisher*

Essays, Manifestos, Statements, Speeches, Maxims,
Epistles, Diaristic Notes, Narrative, Natural Histories,
Poems, Plays, Performances, Ramblings, Revelations and
all such ephemera as may appear necessary to bring society
into a slight tremolo of confusion and fright at least.

Individuals may order through
www.greeninteger.com
Bookstores and libraries should order through our distributor
Consortium Book Sales & Distribution / Ingram Books
(800) 283-3572 / www.cbsd.com

*

SELECTED NEW TITLES

2011

±**Julien Gracq** *The Peninsula* [978-1-933382-39-5] $12.95
Richard Kalich *Penthouse F* [978-1-55713-413-4] $15.95
Ko Un *Himalaya Poems* [978-1-55713-412-7] $13.95
Joe Ross *wordlick* [978-1-55713-415-8] $11.95
†**Nelly Sachs** *Collected Poems 1944-1949* [978-1-933382-57-9] $13.95
†**Tomas Tranströmer** *The Sorrow Gondola* [978-1-933382-44-9] $11.95
    [REPRINT]

2012

Blaise Cendrars *Films without Images* [978-1-933392-55-5] $14.95
Jean Frémon *The Botanical Garden* [978-1-55713-411-0] $13.95
Peter Glassgold *Hwæt!* [978-1-933382-41-8] $12.95
Douglas Messerli *Dark* [978-1-933382-14-2] $12.95
    Reading Films: My International Cinema [978-1-55713-427-1] $29.95
Jules Michelet *The Sea* [1-933382-11-2] $15.95

±**Ivo Michiels** *Book Alpha and Orchis Militaris* [978-1-933382-15-9] $12.95

Yuri Olyesha *Envy* [978-1-931243-12-4] $13.95

2013

Eleanor Antin *Conversations with Stalin* [978-1-55713-420-2] $14.50

Ascher/Straus *Hank Forest's Party* [978-193338-247-0] $12.95

±**Reiner Kunze** *Rich Catch in the Empty Creel* [978-1-933382-24-1] $15.95

Lucebert *The Collected Poems: Volume 1* [978-1-55713-407-3] $15.95

Douglas Messerli *My Year 2003: Voice Without a Voice* [978-1-933382-35-X] $15.95

Xue Di *Across Borders* [978-1-55713-423-3] $12.95

2014

Lee Si-young *Patterns* [978-1-55713-422-6] $11.95

Robert Musil *Three Women* [978-1-55713-419-6] $12.95

2015

Ece Ayhan *A Blind Cat Black* and *Orthodoxies* [978-1-933382-36-4] $11.95

Kim Soo-Bok *Beating on Iron* [978-1-55713-430-1] $12.95

Sigmund Freud / Wilhelm Jensen *Gradiva* and *Delusion and Dream in Wilhelm Jensen's Gradiva* [1-892295-89-X] $13.95 [REPRINT]

Douglas Messerli *My Year 2002: Love, Death, and Transfiguration* [978-1-55713-425-7] $15.95

   My Year 2007: To the Dogs [978-1-55713-424-0] $15.95

   My Year 2008: In the Gap [978-1-55713-462-4] $15.95

Paul van Ostaijen *The First Book of Schmoll* [978-1933382-21-0] $12.95

2016

Jim Gauer *Novel Explosives* [978-1-55713-433-2] $15.95

Douglas Messerli *My Year 2001: Keeping History a Secret* [978-1-

55713-428-8] $15.95

My Year 2009: Facing the Heat [978-1-55713-429-5] $15.95

F. T. Marinetti *The Untameables* [978-1-933382-23-4] $12.95

2017

Régis Bonvicino *Beyond the Wall: New Selected Poems* [978-1-55713-431-8] $12.95

Lee Seong-Bok *Ah—Mouthless Things* [978-1-55713-440-0] $12.95

Lucebert *The Collected Poems: Volume 2* [978-1-55713-434-9] $17.95

Ern Malley *The Darkening Ecliptic* [978-1-55713-439-4] $12.95

Douglas Messerli *My Year 2010: Shadows* [978-1-55713-432-5] $15.95

Steven Moore *My Back Pages* (hardcover) [978-1-55713-437-0] $30.00

2018

Paul Celan *Lightduress* [1-931243-75-1] $19.95 [REPRINT]

Maria Irene Fornes *Abingdon Square* [1-892295-64-4] $19.95 [REPRINT]

Jean Grenier *Islands: Lyrical Essays* [1-892295-95-4] $19.95 [REPRINT]

Atilla Jozsef *A Transparent Lion* [978-1-933382-50-0] $19.95 [REPRINT]

Ko Un *Songs for Tomorrow: A Collection of Poems 1960-2002* [978-1-933382-70-8] $19.95 [REPRINT]

Ten Thousand Lives [1-933382-06-6] $19.95 [REPRINT]

Vladimir Mayakovsky *Vladimir Mayakovsky: A Tragedy* [978-1-55713-444-8] $19.95

Douglas Messerli *My Year 2000: Leaving Something Behind* [978-1-55713-443-1] $15.95

My Year 2011: No One's Home [978-1-55713-442-4] $15.95

Stay [978-1-55713-447-9] $12.95

Steven Moore *My Back Pages* [978-1557134387] $23.00

Toby Olson *The Life of Jesus: An Apocryphal Novel* [978-1-55713-441-7] $19.95

Gertrude Stein *Tender Buttons* [1-931243-42-5] $19.95 [REPRINT]

Three Lives [1-892295-33-4] $19.95 [REPRINT]

Paul Verlaine *The Cursed Poets* [1-931243-15-8] $19.95 [REPRINT]

2019

Adonis *If Only the Sea Could Sleep: Love Poems* [978-1-931243-29-2] $19.95 [REPRINT]

Paul Celan *Threadsuns* [978-1-931243-74-2] $19.95 [REPRINT]

Knut Hamsun *On Overgrown Paths* [978-1-892295-10-1] $19.95 [REPRINT]

José Lezama Lima *A Poetic Order of Excess: Essays on Poets and Poetry* [978-1-892295-98-9] $13.95

Douglas Messerli *My Year 2012: Centers Collapse* [978-1-55713-445-5] $15.95

My Year 2013: Murderers and Angels [978-1-892295-83-5] $15.95

Jean Renoir *An Interview* [978-1-55713-330-4] $19.95 [REPRINT]

Rainer Maria Rilke *Duino Elegies* [978-1-931243-07-0] $19.95 [REPRINT]

Arno Schmidt *The School for Atheists: A Novella = Comedy in 6 Acts* [978-1-892295-96-5] $29.95 [REPRINT]

Oscar Wilde *The Critic as Artist* [978-1-55713-368-7] $19.95 [REPRINT]

2020

Richard Kalich *The Assisted Living Facility Library* [978-1-933382-29-6] $24.95

Murray Pomerance *Grammatical Dreams* [978-1-933382-34-0] $14.95

† Author winner of the Nobel Prize for Literature
± Author winner of the America Award for Literature